FIRE IN THE SKY

On the rise, he scanned the trees along the creek for a campfire. He saw one to the west and began running in that direction. He reached the trees and stopped to regain his breath, his aching lungs heaving in and out. Was he too late?

Finally he spotted what he needed. A double-barreled shotgun leaning against a tree. Trouble was, it was standing in the campfire's light and he was thirty feet from it. A few blasts from it would empty their kegs in a big hurry. It looked like the only solution. He hoped it was heavily loaded.

He rose to a crouch and then broke for it. On the run, he rushed toward the scattergun. In one fell swoop he had it and was on his belly. Aiming down the twin ribs atop the gun barrels, he cocked the right hammer back and blasted away. The first charge of buckshot tore through the barrels lined in a row. A hard impact slammed into his shoulder, but satisfaction cushioned the force. His second shot ripped open two more and started a fire.

"The whiskey!" went up the cry.

"Save it!" But their cursing and shouting were too late . . .

DON'T MISS THESE
ALL-ACTION WESTERN SERIES
FROM THE BERKLEY PUBLISHING GROUP

THE GUNSMITH by J. R. Roberts
Clint Adams was a legend among lawmen, outlaws, and ladies. They called him . . . the Gunsmith.

LONGARM by Tabor Evans
The popular long-running series about U.S. Deputy Marshal Long—his life, his loves, his fight for justice.

SLOCUM by Jake Logan
Today's longest-running action Western. John Slocum rides a deadly trail of hot blood and cold steel.

BUSHWHACKERS by B. J. Lanagan
An all-new series by the creators of Longarm! The rousing adventures of the most brutal gang of cutthroats ever assembled—Quantrill's Raiders.

JAKE LOGAN

SLOCUM AND THE COMANCHE RESCUE

JOVE BOOKS, NEW YORK

SLOCUM AND THE COMANCHE RESCUE

A Jove Book / published by arrangement with
the author

PRINTING HISTORY
Jove edition / October 1997

All rights reserved.
Copyright © 1997 by Jove Publications, Inc.
This book may not be reproduced in whole
or in part, by mimeograph or any other means,
without permission. For information address:
The Berkley Publishing Group,
a member of Penguin Putnam Inc.,
200 Madison Avenue, New York, New York 10016.

The Putnam Berkley World Wide Web site address is
http://www.berkley.com

ISBN: 0-515-12161-4

A JOVE BOOK®
Jove Books are published by The Berkley Publishing Group,
a member of Penguin Putnam Inc.,
200 Madison Avenue, New York, New York 10016.
JOVE and the "J" design are trademarks
belonging to Jove Publications, Inc.

PRINTED IN THE UNITED STATES OF AMERICA

10 9 8 7 6 5 4 3 2 1

1

August 27, 1869

"Quick, come inside my children. The Comanches are coming," the mother hissed from the doorway. Her naked brown-skinned children panicked at her words. They leapt up from their play in the dusty street and ran pell-mell to escape. A boy of perhaps eight, braver than the rest, dared to hesitate for a moment and peer up the road to the east. There was nothing to see, but taking no chances he raced after his brothers and sisters for the sanctuary of their adobe house.

Slocum grinned at the boy's grit as he stood behind the cantina's bat-wing doors; a small cigar in his mouth, he watched for sight of them. Over a month he had waited. At last the terrors of the plains were coming to Cordova, a small village on Espinoza Creek. They were bringing buffalo hides, dried meat, contraband, and even prisoners to trade for cornmeal, flour, knives, gunpowder, and firearms. Kahwadies, the meanest of the mean, would soon ride into the square. Cuerno Verde, Green Horn, led this band. His savage slaughter of white men and Indios ranked him as the worst butcher the caprock had ever known.

Apaches called him harsh names. Green Horn had forced them to retreat and live in the mountains. But not before he had slain hundreds of Apache men, and then, after raping their women, sold them into slavery in Mexico. The Apaches no longer ventured on the short grass and hunted the buffalo, nor did the Navajos, nor did the Utes, who for centuries had come down from the Rockies for such hunts. Green Horn and his Kahwadie Band reigned as the supreme masters of the plains and their staff of life—the bison.

Slocum drew on the cigar and then slowly blew the sharp smoke out his nostrils. He could hear the jingle of small bells and the muffled sounds of horse's hooves coming down the road. The protest of saddle leather and snorts of weary animals carried on the afternoon heat. Then the village cur dogs began to bark from their places of safety as if they would protect the entire village from this band of heathen murderers.

Finally, from his vantage point behind the bat-wing doors, he could see the first of the train. Bare-chested copper-skinned warriors, their sleek, muscled bodies were floured with red dust. The front guard, the bravest ones, were ready to die for their leader. Greasy, sooty, single eagle feathers woven in their braids barely fluttered, black war paint streaked their faces, and silver coins strung on necklaces glinted in the sunlight. Their powerful buffalo horses pranced and danced as if they sensed something important was at hand. Guided by a loop on their lower jaw, they responded to the knee commands of their riders and spun in circles as the Comanches whooped and hollered like insane coyotes.

The crack of their rifle and pistol shots shattered the air and sent the town curs yelping for more cover. Bloodthirsty war cries and the yipping of the riders made the hair on the back of Slocum's neck rise as they raced around the fountain. He stood with his boots planted and watched the procession spill into the village.

Behind the front riders on a great paint horse came the fat king of the Kahwadie. His ponderous belly, like a huge red sack, hung over his breechcloth. A fancy quill vest was open, exposing his balloon-sized gut. Two deep-set slits of glinting coal in his bloated face, his cruel eyes missed few details. Greasy hair bushed above the intricately beaded headband that sprouted the huge painted horn in the center of his forehead. Green Horn had arrived in Cordova.

Beyond the bat-wing doors, other Kahwadie passed Slocum's vantage point. Their squaws came next afoot, leading horses pulling travois, the poles hissing on the ground under the heavy loads piled on them. Comanche women by tradition were not interesting to look at, and must never attract other men. Hair cut short and irregular with a knife, a Comanche woman dared not smile at anyone or anything lest her husband see her and misconceive her purpose. Taught to stare away and always keep her head down, they brought the trade goods on travois and packhorses into the village square.

He watched carefully, knowing the last in the procession were the prisoners. More warriors on horseback rode by, leading three men. Ropes around their necks, they walked, single file, their bare skin blistered black from the summer sun. Half alive, no doubt Cordova was their first sight of civilization in months. They must think this adobe village was heaven.

Next, six young Indian girls dressed in rags, riding double on poor ponies, passed Slocum. They were prisoners too. He wondered if his time had been wasted, waiting all this while. A blond-haired girl in her late teens came behind them, riding a wind-broken pony. Her hands tied in front of her, the llano sun had turned her fair skin to a saddle-leather brown. Could this be Myra McChristian?

He drew on his cigar and the winy juices from the stub filled his mouth. It had gone out while he'd been busy scrutinizing the parade. Still watching the show in the street, he struck alive a lucifer on the seat of his pants and then torched the cigar. Once more the strong, smooth smoke came from the butt to his tongue. If she was the McChristian girl, he had spent his time well.

He still had to buy her from them. They would be tough traders. He had been warned by the village *mayordomo*, Aguliar Gomez. The Comanches knew how to barter. For over three hundred years his people had taught them how, and they had come in the spring and late summer to trade at Cordova. The owner of the place, Elandro, hurriedly closed the main doors.

"No sale to the Comanche?" Slocum asked.

"No, señor. No sales, they go crazy when they get drunk. No one is allowed to sell them liquor. We treasure our women and children too much."

Slocum had seen enough anyway. He walked over to the bar as the war cries and shooting holes in the sky continued out front. The Indians intended to show their prowess to these villagers.

"They will soon calm down and start trading," Elandro said to reassure Slocum. He leaned on the bar top, a corn-shuck cigarette in the corner of his dark lips.

"They ever come in here?" Slocum asked.

"No, it is never allowed."

"What about the slaves? When will they sell them?"

"Tonight, it is like an auction. Don Lucas, he will be in charge."

"The man from Santa Fe who arrived a few days ago?" Slocum had seen the man of obvious means who had arrived a few days earlier with three bodyguards. There was not much in the small village he did not know about, including the trappers who had set up camp on the stream east of town. A rowdy bunch, but they'd pretty much stayed to themselves so far.

"Why is this Don Lucas in charge?"

"He buys most of the slaves."

"What does he do with them?"

"Ransoms those that he can. The others gladly work out the cost of their redemption."

"He must be very rich?"

"He makes much money. Once a rancher from Chihuahua, he paid him a thousand gold eagles for his daughter's return."

"Whew, that is a lot of money. Do others come and bid?"

"Oh, *sí*. There is a yellow-haired lady from Albuquerque comes to buy *putas* for her house. And sometimes mountain men, they come and buy wives. Not so many anymore."

"How do they know when to come?"

The smaller man shrugged as he put his cigarette out in a broken pottery base. He coughed deeply, cleared his throat, and spoke. "They find out somehow. Is the one you look for out there?"

Slocum nodded as the man poured him a shot of whiskey. The auction would be quite spirited if a white girl if was included. Perhaps he didn't have enough money or goods to buy her. What then? He would cross that bridge when the time came.

He left the saloon when the excitement in the square settled down. Outside, he hoped his clothing was not too conspicuous. He wore leather britches, a fringed buckskin shirt, and a flat-brimmed hat with a chin string. His pants were tucked into his Apache-style boots, their rounded toes less conspicuous than the pointed type.

The .31 Colt in a holster on his hip, he considered his

appearance that of a typical resident. He strode off, watching the Comanche women busy unrolling buffalo hides, some stiff and green, some soft and subtle. All the bucks had retired to squat in the shade. Without being obvious, he could not see the girl anywhere among the over fifty horses and various tradesmen crowding the small square.

Under the cottonwoods along the creek on his way to the small hut he rented, Slocum noticed that the usual brown children who splashed and squealed in the creek were not present. His small adobe was ahead. He could see the buckskin horse and the roan in the pen out back. They'd assured him that the Comanches stole little when they came to trade. He would hate them to take his good horses while he was busy trying to buy her. But everything in life was a chance.

He paused on the slope and looked back at the stream. There were no women washing clothes at the rock riffle either, none carrying water in olla on their heads from the well. He could hear the grasshoppers' clicking, a few mourning doves in the cottonwoods, and the wind rustling the leaves.

The people of the village did not take this Comanche visit as casually as they had told Slocum they did. The bland shrug that his landlord, Miguel Rosa, gave him when he asked about the Kahwadie coming was deceptive. "They come all the time," Miguel had said. Obviously, the people of Cordova respected as well as feared the rulers of the plains.

Slocum pushed open the thick door to his hut. It was time to ready his items of trade. How high would the bidding go? There was no way to know. The madam from Albuquerque—no telling what she'd give for a white girl. The girl would be at a premium in this land of brown skins. And this Don Lucas, was he scoundrel or a hero? What reputable person ran a business ransoming white captives?

Had he wasted almost two months by riding to Cordova

and then waiting for the Comanches to come? No, somehow he would succeed at the evening auction. It was a damn long ride back to Abilene. The girl's father, Jim Ed, would soon be there with his herd, and even after he sold it he planned to remain until Slocum returned with his daughter.

He'd promised the man nothing. For two hundred dollars and the ransom cost, he would try to bring her back if she was alive. Strong rumors out of Fort Griffin said she was a captive of the Kahwadies. But hearsay across five hundred miles of Texas meant little. Her condition had amazed him after almost seven months with them. He'd expected worse and told Jim Ed to be prepared for an Indian grandson. The man's steel-blue eyes never wavered.

"Bring her back, Slocum. My wife and sons are dead. They killed them. She's all I've got left."

The memory of Jim Ed's serious expression and concern for his daughter's return, even if it meant her bringing back a bastard grandson, was still strong as Slocum removed new rifles from their case. He wrapped his trade items in a Navajo blanket. They would be an armload, but he wanted to impress his competition. He wondered what else he could use to buy her if his weapons weren't enough. There was no way for him to wire Jim Ed for more money; he was on the cattle trail somewhere between the Trinity River and Abilene. He would somehow have to do this buying his own way.

There was plenty of time until nightfall and the auction. His hat on a rack, he stretched his tall frame out on the bed and stared at the stick and mud waddle ceiling. This was a bidding war that he couldn't afford to lose. He closed his eyes and tried to nap. Flies buzzed around him and the afternoon heat made him uncomfortable. The picture of her sitting that horse, looking straight ahead, made his stomach turn sour.

2

Torches lighted the town square in an eerie orange light. Men loitered about the outer edge, talking softly in small groups. The platform in the center had been constructed after he went to his hut. It was surrounded by flaming pitch lights. The shadows on the buildings looked like giants as men crossed the square.

"Ah, Señor Slocum," Elandro said, joining him. "Soon we will know the price of humans, no?"

"I have seen those men in buckskin before," Slocum said, indicating the three bearded men who leaned on their long Hawkins rifles. He'd known plenty of those who lived on the frontier. They hunted buffalo and traded the hides.

"They're the Updikes and their men. Oh, look, there's the coach." Elandro pointed to the closed carriage. A black man stepped down and opened the door. A woman

8

emerged in a blue ruffled hoop dress, drawing everyone's eye. Her curled hair, piled high, was golden, and her oval face strikingly haunting as she ignored the stares and quietly spoke to the black man.

"What's her name?" Slocum asked.

"Thelma Van Doorne."

She was much younger than he had expected and a damn sight more attractive, though he knew she had a heart as cold as an iceberg when it came to business.

Soon seated in a canvas and wood folding chair under an umbrella, she looked ready to hold court fifty feet from the empty platform. Well armed, two men flanking her provided protection should the need arise.

Don Lucas rode in from the east on a mane-tossing, dancing black horse. His entourage of three men wearing bandoliers and obviously *pistoleros,* they followed him into the square. After he dismounted close to Madame Van Doorne, he swept off his hat and bowed for her.

She acknowledged him with a nod and they made small talk, Slocum could not hear their words. Then Don Lucas gave his reins to one of his men and went off, no doubt to find the Comanches.

"So everyone is here," Elandro said, folding his arms over his chest.

"What are they bringing up?" he asked as one of the mountain men led a pair of pack mules into the square.

"Two mules loaded with whiskey." A look of disbelief clouded the barkeeper's face.

"Whiskey?"

"Oh, it is bad too." The man shook his head and made a face. "That stuff is close to horse piss."

"Must be terrible if you think it's that bad," Slocum said, considering the man's bar stock of liquor as less than good.

"Here comes the *mayordomo,* Aguilar Gomez." Elandro pointed to the short, thickset man who was the politico force in the community, judge and administrator. During his stay Slocum had seen this man at work: A drunk who had beaten his wife was hauled before him, Gomez gave him the choice of her beating him or paying a fine. The man paid.

The mayor's look of determination as he headed for the squaw men was enough to draw attention from the gathered crowd who started whispering to one another.

"Take that poison and go!" Gomez ordered in Spanish. He pointed to the north. "We don't trade whiskey to *Indios* in this village."

"By damn." The biggest of the three spat tobacco in the dust between them as a warning. Gripping his rifle barrel, he looked ready to fly into a rage. "Them damn Comanche ain't against it."

"This is my village. Go out there and trade with them on the plains." The man threw his arm to the east to indicate where they could sell their rotgut. "You will trade in my village by my rules."

"Comanches live by few rules," Elandro informed Slocum as they listened to the argument. "Those men would not dare go out on the caprock and trade with Green Horn. He would take their whiskey from them and make them slaves—if he didn't kill them."

"They're backing down." Slocum folded his arms over his chest as he saw the mayor press his point. Obviously, they weren't as tough as they acted.

"*Sí*, they don't want to be barred from trading at all."

Slocum agreed as he studied the blond woman seated regally in the chair. Tall and willowy, she looked as if she had all the time in the world.

The Updikes led their mules away. On the stage, several squaws began to cover a large chair with fine robes and Navajo blankets. Soon the great balloon figure of Green Horn came out on the platform and a silence fell over the crowd. His diamond-hard eyes searched the square before he dropped his enormous butt on the seat.

Surrounded by his lieutenants, he motioned for one to bend over to tell him something in his ear.

"He has never been wounded in warfare, they say," Elandro whispered.

"Big enough target," Slocum said. "The man must live a charmed life."

The Indian girl captives came first. Roughly hauled up by the Kawahdie men, they stood hangdog in rags, filthy and their hair matted. Slocum looked beyond the pitiful sight to try to find the white girl.

The first to sell, a girl in her early teens was shoved forward. Don Lucas stepped on the stage and nodded to Green Horn as if asking for his approval to begin the sale. The king motioned for him to go ahead, and the auction began.

"Five gold eagles," Don Lucas said, "is the opening bid. A healthy young girl."

The tallest of the guards reached down and pulled her dress up to expose her belly and the dark seam of black pubic hair. Roughly he half spun her around. He made sure that all could see her features, then he let go of her skirt and stepped back. The girl remained frozen, her dress still bunched up, exposing her, but she did nothing. Finally, like a heavy curtain, the skirt fell and covered her.

"Seven!" one of the squaw men said, and punctuated his offer with a spit in the dust.

"Ten," Mrs. Van Doorne said.

"Twelve," the man added.

"Fifteen," she said.

"By damn, Ernie, that rich bitch may make you pay for that little love kitten tonight," the leader said, then he and his Ernie laughed aloud.

"Twenty," Ernie said, acting unruffled by the jab.

"Twenty-five," she said.

A silence settled as everyone looked at the mountain man for his bid. He scowled, spat, and then shook his head as if he never wanted the girl in the first place. "Let her have her."

Don Lucas turned to the big chief, who acted disinterested in the entire process. Whatever was said was not audible to Slocum. But the amount must have been acceptable, for the chief agreed with a grunt and one of the bucks ushered the girl off the stage to stand beside the woman. A black man counted out the coins and put them in his hand before he released her.

Thelma Van Doorne had a blanket spread on the ground and indicated for the girl to sit down beside her. Cross-legged and numb, she obeyed, perhaps not realizing she had traded one form of slavery for another. This one would be easier in many ways than life among the Comanches as an outcast, but nonetheless serfdom in Slocum's eyes.

A small Indian girl of ten sold for two double eagles to a couple who, Elandro said, had no children. Then a twelve-year-old went to Mrs. Van Doorne for seven double eagles, and joined her other purchase on the fine blanket.

"Damn, Ernie, are you saving your money for that white bitch? She'll cost a whole damn winter's buffalo hunting," the big man said out loud to his companion.

Another young Indian girl sold to a local couple as a servant, according to Elandro, the price less than five double eagles. Slocum was busy thinking how his own goods on the buckskin horse might impress the big man more than money.

The first male prisoner was shoved to the center of the stage. Hardly twenty years old, he stood stoop-shouldered, a rag around his waist. The big buck stepped over and raised the cloth to show her that he had all his privates and then grinned, as if taunting Mrs. Van Doorne.

She acted as if she had not seen a thing. But the rest of the Comanches were laughing at his action and pointing at each other's breechclouts. No doubt they wanted everyone to know that theirs measured larger than the boy's.

"Do you have any kinfolk who will pay for your ransom?" Don Lucas asked the man.

"Naw." The captive shook his head. "All of them were killed."

"Five double eagles." Don Lucas started the bidding.

In the end, Lucas bought the man for that sum. After the sale and Lucas's explanation, Green Horn looked disappointed and angry at the amount paid for him. He spoke sharply to his lieutenants, and they agreed with head bobs.

Then the chief motioned for Lucas to come over. They had a rapid exchange in Spanish over the big man's displeasure with the low price. Lucas acted as if that was all he could pay. Green Horn made the sign of cutting his own throat with the side of his hand. Obviously he was unwilling to sell any more male captives for such a low price.

"Ten double eagles shall be the starting price for the other two," Don Lucas announced. "Green Horn says he will personally kill them if they are worth no more than that."

"Do you intend to buy them?" Mrs. Van Doorne asked him openly.

"It is a lot of money for ones I cannot ransom," he said, looking around uneasily, as if he felt unsafe with his company on the stage.

"If no one else bids, you buy one and I will take the other," she said, disgusted with his lack of spirit and compassion.

"A deal," he said. "Is there anyone here who can afford one of these other men?"

A series of head shakes around the square answered him. "Fine, then the lady and I shall buy the other two."

He turned and talked to the chief again, who begrudgingly gave his approval.

"Now the one that we have waited for," Lucas said as

if released from some burden. "This young lady is from Texas. Her father's a great rancher. His name is Bartlett."

No, the man had said it wrong. McChristian, not Bartlett. Was she the wrong girl, or had she somehow forgotten her name? Myra McChristian. She was the only white captive close to her description. Had he spent two months in vain waiting for her? Was she even alive?

He frowned at the actions onstage. What was the big buck doing with her? He had forced her to bend over until her hands touched the platform, then he reached down and drew back his breechclout. He tossed her dress up over her, baring her slender, snow-white butt, and then he stepped close behind her. Directing his rod into her, his hunching muscular butt pumping against her had an obvious purpose. *The son of a bitch was violating her!* Slocum's hand tightened on the butt of his Colt. The indecent bastard needed to be shot.

A wide grin filled the buck's face as he pulled her hard against his hips, then he strained with a loud grunt and forced himself deep inside her. Finished, he stepped back. His stiff rod dripped with his slick fluids. It shined in the red light of the torches.

"Now she is ready. You can sell her," he said in Spanish to the pale-faced Don Lucas. The rest of Comanches on the platform laughed out loud to mock their wide-eyed audience, then they whooped over the matter. Green Horn nodded his approval from his throne.

Slocum's heart pounded in his chest. Chills ran up his jaw and tightened the skin on his face as he fought for control. He removed his hand from the gun butt and dried his wet palm on the side of his pants.

"Who is that sumbitch?" he finally managed to ask Elandro.

"Lightning Strikes."

"It may strike him soon," Slocum said as the buck jerked her upright with a hand full of her hair. The man deserved—no, he needed—killing. Slocum closed his eyes to the audacity of the cruel savage's actions. Tears streamed down the girl's dirt-caked face.

"Let the bidding begin at fifty dollars," Don Lucas said.

3

"Fifty double eagles," the mountain man shouted.

"Wait, sir," Slocum said aloud to Don Lucas. "I have a better offer than money." He led the buckskin horse forward. Then he peeled back the canvas cover and drew out a gold-plated breech Winchester. The sight of it awed his audience. They did not know it was not solid gold, nor was he going to explain that by the time the finish wore off, exposing the brass beneath he intended to be many miles away.

"I say, two of these many-shot rifles for her and four more for the blond girl, Myra McChristian." His hunch was they had the girl, unless she had died. It was a dangerous ploy, but so was trading with them in the first place.

"Hell, anyone knows you can buy them damn—" the

16

mountain man Ernie started to interrupt, but was cut off by the fierce look Slocum shot at him.

"Hush your mouth, mister, or I'll bust out every tooth in your empty head. We ain't talking about your grunting pleasure here. We're talking about two girls' lives." Slocum looked at the man as hard as he could, then satisfied his threat had worked, he slowly turned back to face the Indians onstage.

"How many guns?" Lightning Strikes demanded.

"Two for her!" Slocum held up two fingers. "Four for Myra McChristian."

"No Myra," Lightning said, shaking his head as he squatted, eager to examine the Winchester.

"Four for Myra," Slocum said again before he handed over the rifle.

The big Indian took the rifle and carefully ran his hand over the smooth oily finish, then he unlatched and latched the lever, snapping the hammer down hard. The loud click made many in the crowd jump back.

Lightning Strikes held the rifle high. His action drew ear-shattering war cries from the others as they crowded close to see the prize. Slocum could not see the expression on their chief's face, for the braves were gathered closely around him. Finally they parted and the chief was on his feet. He padded across the stage, the rifle in his hand, motioning for the other long gun.

Slocum shook his head. "Two for her." He made the sign with his fingers. "Four for Myra." He held up four digits for him.

The big man leaned over to hear Lightning Strikes translate the words in his ear. Next he straightened, not taking his cold glare from Slocum, then he walked back to speak in guttural Comanche with the others. Their conference was long, and Slocum wished he knew more of their talk. Finally Don Lucas was summoned and the Spanish flowed, but still the words were not clear enough for him to understand. The man backed out and then he walked to the edge of the platform, where Slocum stood.

"They say they don't have this other woman that you ask for."

"Tell them they are dogs who lie. They don't want to give her up. A great spirit told me she was in the Kahwadie camp." His mention of a spirit might unnerve them. They weren't afraid of much, but magic counted high with Indians.

"Man, tell them that yourself." Lucas pleaded. He looked uneasily over his shoulder, then back at Slocum.

"You speak Spanish better than I do," he said, tossing his head for Don Lucas to continue.

"You may get us all killed," Don Lucas said with a wary shake of his head. "You don't know who you are dealing with."

"I know that they have the other girl."

"Jesus, man, this is too dangerous," he hissed.

"Tell him!" His patience was wearing thin. He scowled at the man until he shrugged in defeat and finally went to deliver his message to Green Horn.

Slocum's breath came heavily as he considered what he must do next. He'd come this far, and he wasn't settling for going back without Myra or learning her fate. Everything had a price with these people. But was his offer enough to get them to budge?

"I like your style," Mrs. Van Doorne said with a laugh from her chair beside him.

"Another place and time perhaps?"

"Yes, if you live that long," she agreed.

There was no time to answer her. Lightning Strikes came dragging the Bartlett girl to the edge of the platform.

"Two Yellow boys?" he demanded.

"Two for her. Four—"

"That one will be here by the dawn," the scowling buck said in good English.

Slocum turned and reached back for the other rifle. The

buck and his ward had leapt to the ground. He shoved her at him when Slocum turned to face them with the other half of his payment.

Lightning Strikes took the rifle, but his savage expression was that of a man obsessed. Without a word he leapt up on the stage and, screaming, held the second rifle over his head as he waded back to his chief.

"Come along, girls," Mrs. Van Doorne said, motioning for the two to go with the black man. "I'd heard there was blond girl with them," she said to Slocum, who held the Bartlett girl protectively in his left arm and watched the Comanche warily. "I guess you have bought her too."

"I hope I have," he said, tight-lipped, not trusting them for a second.

"Watch your backside," she said, rising to her feet in a rustle of tafetta. "Those grubby mountain men may get you next, that's if the Comanches don't decide they don't like the deal and decide to take her back."

"You can think of lots of nice things," he said to her, keeping the Comanches onstage in his view.

"I would say, sir—"

"Slocum's my name."

"I would say, Mr. Slocum, that you have taken a tightrope to walk."

"Ma'am, I stay on one."

"For the girl's sake, I hope you manage to cross to the other side." Her skirts in hand, she headed for her carriage. The two girls and the man, wearing clothes her black servant supplied, had already gone to the coach.

"Good-bye, Slocum," she said, pausing before climbing aboard. "And do come by my place. We will play less dangerous games and have much more fun, I can assure you."

"I shall, ma'am." He hugged the sobbing girl and spoke to reassure her. "You'll be fine. We have to be careful leaving here—"

"Come you must stay tonight in my cantina, the mayor

says you must not go to your *casa*." Elandro took him by the arm. "This is very serious what you did tonight. The mayor, he is very upset. He fears that the Updikes may try to trade them their whiskey. We must all pray to God that the Comanches don't kill us for double-crossing them."

"Double-crossing them?" he shouted as the cantina owner led away his buckskin horse toward his place. "Young lady, I'm sorry. But I will get you to your people." He glanced back at the stage, where the Kahwadies were huddled as he half carried her with him. *And I will repay Lightning Strikes for what he did to you tonight. I promise you that.*

"How will we get away from them?" she asked as they reached the dark alley. "They will wait for us, especially if they give you Myra."

"Myra is with them?" He felt elated at his newfound knowledge. "Why is it a bigger problem if we get Myra?"

"She is one of Green Horn's wives."

"Oh, hell, no wonder he was in such a stew over letting her go. Here is the door, go inside. Elandro will take care of you."

"Where are you going?" she cried, clinging to his arm to stop him.

"I have business. It may mean whether we live or die. Elandro will take care of you," he said, prying her fingers from his arm.

"No, I'll never see you again," she pleaded. Tears welled in her eyes.

"Stay here," he ordered. He needed to destroy some whiskey, and his time was short. Once free of her grasp, he half ran down the empty alley. The Updikes must be camped somewhere north along the creek. He must locate them before the Comanches got hold of their firewater.

On the rise, he scanned the trees along the creek for a campfire. He saw one to the west and began running in

that direction and looking across the star-lit sage and
grassland for any sign of a rider's silhouette.

He reached the trees and stopped to regain his breath,
his aching lungs heaving in and out. Was he too late?
Finally he recovered his breath and moved through the
cottonwoods; the firelit area west of him looked promis-
ing.

"Hey, chief, you want whiskey. We got plenty whiskey," Ernie Updike said, and clapped Lightning Strikes
on the shoulder. He handed the small keg to the buck as
the firelight glinted off his sleek copper skin. From his
place beside the cottonwood trunk, Slocum could see the
two of them and hear every word from his vantage point.

"This plenty good!" Lightning Strikes said, and
grinned at them.

"Bring your chief. We can get plenty gold rifles and
whiskey for you," Ernie said.

"Bring plenty Comanche," Lightning Strikes said, and
hoisted the keg up to drink more from the spigot.

Slocum stood pressed hard to the tree's rough bark.
Then he dropped to all fours and started making his way
around the camp. The Updikes had left him no option; he
had to destroy their liquor at any cost.

A large hound barked in his ear, close enough to deafen
him. The dog's panting tongue stuck in his face stopped
his heart, but the hound acted as if he expected to find
men crawling around his portion of the camp. A few pats
on the head and the hound began thumping his tail in the
dust. He dropped down again and acted satisfied. Slocum
went on.

Finally he spotted what he needed. A double-barreled
shotgun leaning against a tree. Trouble was, it was standing in the campfire's light and he was thirty feet from it.
A few blasts from it would empty their kegs in a big
hurry. It looked like the only solution. He hoped it was
heavily loaded.

"Where did that damn Slocum go afterward?" He listened to the Updikes' conversation as he considered the weapon and how he could reach it without being seen.

"Gawdamn if I know—sumbitch vanished with that girl too."

"He's probably in Santa Fe by now."

"Naw, there's another white bitch with them that he wants worse."

"The sumbitch offering them damn Comanches a Yellow Boy rifle. Two of them for her. Why, I can buy them for fifty bucks. Damn, I hate him. I could've had that bitch for my very own tonight."

"Stop worrying about damn nooky and get your minds on business. We're making a big deal with Green Horn tonight."

They were distracted enough for Slocum to chance a dash for the shotgun. He rose to a crouch and then broke for it. On the run, he rushed toward the scattergun. In one fell swoop he had it and was on his belly. Aiming down the twin ribs atop the gun barrels, he cocked the right hammer back and blasted away. The first charge of buckshot tore through the barrels lined in a row. A hard impact slammed into his shoulder, but satisfaction cushioned the force. His second shot ripped open two more and started a fire.

"The whiskey!"

"Save it!" But their cursing and shouting were too late.

Slocum was already on his feet. He tossed the gun aside and had begun slashing the picket ropes of their horses and mules with his large knife, sending off the scared animals.

Then the explosion of a keg of black powder added to the confusion. He hadn't planned on that. In a leap he slipped onto a small horse and, lying flat on its back, made it trot after the mules to the east.

The Updikes were railing at the inferno, and then black powder explosions lighted the sky behind him. He clung tighter to the pony's neck and urged it after the mules, who were kicking their heels, breaking wind, and racing to flee the great booms behind them.

At last he slipped from the small horse and, keeping low, headed for the dark outline of the village on the rise. The animals hurried on eastward. It would be days before the mountain men gathered all of them.

His plan to simply trade for Jim Ed's daughter had not gone as smoothly as he had planned. He'd come to barter for the girl and then take her back. At the moment he had another girl and could only wonder if the fat chief would keep his word for four rifles and deliver his own bride in exchange.

"Yes, who is out there?" Elandro asked from behind the door when he knocked.

"Slocum, quick, open up."

"Did anyone follow you?" The man peered up and down the dark alley.

"No. How is the girl?"

"Asleep. What was all that noise we heard and the fireworks?"

"I think Updike's whiskey and powder blew up."

"How come?" Elandro narrowed his brown eyes in the flickering candlelight.

"Damned if I know. Must have been real firewater. Where can I lie down for a while?"

"On the roof is a hammock. It is cool up there." He tossed his head toward the ladder that went through a hole in the ceiling.

"Good, you'd better get some sleep yourself."

"How can I with all these Comanches out there?"

"Hell, they went to bed too." Slocum waved to him and began to climb the ladder to the roof. Once he was on top, he searched the starlit sky. The moon hadn't come up yet. He headed for the hammock with sleep on his mind.

4

Dawn tried to peek over the hills to the east. Rubbing the three-day stubble on his face, Slocum attempted to scrub the numbness from his brain as he sat on the edge of the hammock and listened to a rooster crow. He closed his dry eyes to the events of the past twenty-four hours; finally he managed to stand up and stretch his stiff frame.

Whatever this day brought he probably deserved. His wild plans to try to outsmart the Kahwadies may not have worked. He still lacked the McChristian girl, and could not trust the Kahwadie to keep their word. Comanche truth was what suited them.

He descended the ladder into the interior of the dark cantina and living quarters. In the shadowy light of the room, he saw the Bartlett girl sitting up on a pallet, wrapped in a thick woven cotton blanket.

24

"Good morning," he said, and squatted on his boot heels before her.

"Good morning," she managed in a dry voice. Her dust-caked face was still streaked from crying the night before. It held a blankness he had seen before on other captives. No doubt the stress of their indecent treatment at the hands of their captors forced them to withdraw into an inner world. Also her hair had been hacked short with a knife in their fashion. She almost looked like a typical Comanche woman.

"We'll get you a bath and some clothing today."

She nodded, holding the blanket tight around her.

"What do they call you?"

"You mean—them?"

"No." He didn't give a damn what the Comanches called her. "What do your own people at home call you."

"Laura Beth."

"I'm Slocum."

"I know, he told me last night." She motioned toward the front of the cantina.

"I will take you home as soon as I can. If they bring Myra today, we'll get under way."

"But they will only take her back and probably kill you." She looked ready to bawl.

"They may be tough, but they're not omnipotent. Where do your people live?"

"Texas, near the Brazos."

"We will find them."

She had turned away and was crying. Her thin shoulders shook under the blanket. He reached over and patted her on the back to reassure her that nothing bad would happen to her again if he could help it. The crying might be good for her; sometimes tears washed away a lot of past trials. It would be all right; she would feel better after a bath, clean and in real clothing, instead of rags.

"I'm going to find a woman to help you," he said, and rose to his feet.

Slocum's other trade items were piled on the bar when he entered the barroom. He spotted Elandro sleeping in a chair with a sawed-off shotgun across his lap before the barred front doors.

Behind the bar, Slocum helped himself to a double shot of his whiskey. Then he cleared his throat so loud, the little man bolted up in the chair.

"Oh, it was only you," the man said with a shake of his head.

"We need some food."

"Ah, we can go down the alley and Maria Constallas, she will feed us."

"She up this early?" He had eaten there before and knew the woman slightly.

"Ah, *sí*, she is always up with the chickens. How is the girl you bought?" He motioned to the back room.

"Fine. Sad, but you would be too."

"I think my heart would quit if I was one of their prisoners." He rose and crossed the room to set the short scattergun on the bar.

"Trouble is, most hearts aren't that bad. Let's go find some food."

"We can go out the back way." Elandro tossed his head to the rear.

"I'll get the girl." Slocum considered the shotgun before him and then handed it to Elandro. "We'd better take it along."

"Oh, *sí*, the Comanche are coming back today. I almost forgot."

The girl used the blanket against the coolness and to hide her shabby dress. She walked beside him, her head down. When she was better, he would teach her how to walk straight again. Returned captives who did not shed their Indian ways were targets for being ridiculed and branded by cruel people. They became objects of curiosity like a captured albino badger. Laura Beth needed to arrive at her home a white woman, not a subjected Comanche squaw.

Maria's small café held several customers, who turned to look at the three and then turned back to their plates. The usual rich aroma in the place of meat and fresh bread made Slocum hungrier. They took seats at a small table.

"What do you want to eat, Laura?" he asked

She shrugged, obviously very self-conscious in the crowded place.

"Ignore these people," he whispered. "They are only trees in a forest. Today is the first day of your new life. Do you hear me?"

"Yes." Her head bobbed.

The side of his hand under her chin, he raised her face up. "Laura Beth Bartlett, you begin to act like her again."

"Yes," she agreed, but avoided looking at anyone.

"We want eggs and meat," he said to the young woman who came to wait on them, indicating the order was for the two of them.

"Me too," Elandro said.

In a moment, a short woman in her thirties wish ample hips and a full face came and stood before their table.

"This is the child from the Comanches?" she asked.

"Yes, this is Laura Beth," Slocum said as Elandro rushed to introduce him to Maria.

"I have seen them in here and around the village for many days," she said. "Is there anything I can do for her?"

"Yes, after we eat. A bath and get her some fine clothes," Slocum said. "I can pay you."

"The bath is nothing, señor. The clothing I will find, some good ones, I have several daughters. Something nice will fit her."

He could see the motherly compassion in the woman's brown eyes. She spoke in Spanish to the girl, assuring her that she would soon be a new person. Laura only nodded that she had heard her.

"Señor, come quick," a man said from the doorway. "The Comanches are here in the plaza with another girl for you."

Slocum had to tell Laura to stay and eat. She looked apprehensive, but remained seated.

"I may have a second bath customer," he said to Maria as he rose to leave. She agreed.

"God be with you, amigo," she said after him, and made the sign of the cross over her breasts.

"You need this?" Elandro asked, offering him the shotgun.

"No, I must try to make the trade in good faith."

On his rawhide soles, he ran down the alley, inside the cantina through the back door, and he soon held an armload of weapons and was headed outside again.

He could see the dancing ponies from the corner of the building where he stopped. Sunlight glinted off their copper bodies. The three riders swung their mounts around as if searching for something to pounce upon. All prime athletes in suburb condition, with lean, muscle-corded bellies. Their long thin braids whipped around, the supreme buffalo hunter and soldier.

There was no room in their camp for the old or afflicted. If a warrior was hurt and permanently crippled, unable to continue, he chose suicide, for there was no place in their lifestyle for anyone unable to perform, including their women. No old females lounged around in the Comanche lodges either, their wombs barren with age and unable to work. They went out on the prairie and sat down to wait for death to take them. It usually came swiftly at the hands of an enemy, wolves, or starvation; the Comanche was a young society.

That was why they took so many females captives to replenish their numbers. Slocum knew this as he undid the thong on his Colt's hammer. The Yellow Boys lined along the adobe wall, he stepped out, arms folded, and waited for their attention. In an instant Lightning Strikes drove his horse forward in a great surge and stopped him only inches from Slocum's face.

"The girl?" he asked, unfazed by the man's actions.

"Who are you?" Lightning Strikes demanded.

"A man who comes for the girl."

"You are not her father or brother?"

Slocum shook his head.

The buck still acted uncertain about his purpose, but shouted and waved for the others to bring her over to them. Slocum could see them leading a small roan pony. A figure gripped the mane as another buck moved in and quirted the reluctant pony on the butt.

"Myra McChristian?" Slocum asked her.

"Yes." The emotionless, hollow face with sunken eyes nodded woodenly. She sat huddled in a filthy dress. Her bare legs were dirty and scarred from whipping, no doubt.

"The rifles!" the Comanche demanded.

Slocum nodded, and then he stepped to the side of the building to get them. He handed them one at a time to Lightning Strikes, who passed them to the others. There was something afoot with the three bucks. He could feel it. They were a mobile force capable of striking and fleeing at the blink of an eye. When he handed out the third rifle, he thought he understood what they planned.

The one holding her pony's lead carried one rifle. If they double-crossed him, they figured with her trailing behind them on the pony that he wouldn't dare shoot at them. Then, knowing what their next move would be, he handed Lightning Strikes the final weapon. Holding two rifles, the leader was almost harmless—in his greed for the fancy rifles, he would hardly dare drop one of them.

Slocum rushed in, took her by the waist, and pulled her slender form off the pony. The buck ready to lead her away looked shocked. Slocum dragged her back toward the building, drawing his Colt at the same time and facing the three men.

"Get ready to run between the buildings behind us," he told the quaking girl in his arm as he released her. "They can't get a horse through there."

She didn't answer, but he could hear her breathing beside him. He shoved her with his left hand. "Run!" he ordered.

Without a word she obeyed, and he dared not look, his right hand filled with the small Dragoon .31. He searched them for what they planned to do next. The new rifles were empty. He held all the aces for the moment.

"Someday I will kill you for this!" Lightning Strikes said through his teeth.

"Leave now or you will die here." Slocum motioned them away with his hexagon barrel.

They whirled their horses and, screaming, rode from the plaza. He stood for a moment and let the tension drain from his body. It was over for them.

Armed men came rushing into the square, the mayor among them. Slocum holstered the pistol and turned to look for the girl. She hesitated in the space between the two stores.

"Myra?"

"Yes. Oh, thank God, you have saved me," she cried. "I couldn't warn you of their plans." She ran to him and buried her face in his chest.

"Somehow I suspected that was the case," he said, drawing a deep breath to settle himself as he hugged her to reassure his latest ward that her tragic captivity was over.

"Señor, you have the girl. And you also saved our village by burning the whiskey last night," the mayor said, backed by his armed defenders. "We knew only you could have done such a thing. Those men will be barred from ever trading here ever again."

He nodded that he'd heard the man's promise as he held her. *Jim Ed, I have your daughter. A tough two-hundred-dollar job.*

5

"Two women to care for." Elandro shook his head as if the matter were very serious for him. "How will you take them back to their people?"

"Probably find a wagon train or a stagecoach at Santa Fe returning east and put them on it. When they get to Abilene, Jim Ed can take the two of them back to Texas."

"So you ride for Santa Fe?"

"Soon as they get through bathing, getting their new clothes. The mayor has found me another horse and saddle."

"Oh, all the villagers are very grateful to you. Will you stop and see the yellow-haired one?" Elandro grinned knowingly.

"Might do that. She did say she played games less dangerous than last night." He smiled at the prospect of some bare-ass fun in a feather bed with the tall blonde.

"I would watch my backside, señor. Those mountain men are not going to like that you blew up all their whiskey and gunpowder as well as bought the white women they came to buy."

"Have you heard if they rode on?" he asked, considering the threat and where they might be.

"They rode on, but who knows how far? The major, he ordered all of them from our valley, but they could ride to the next one and then come right back." Elandro shrugged and then he went to wait on two customers down the bar.

Slocum considered the man's words. The Updikes were not going to take his attack lightly. The loss had probably bankrupted them for a while. However it would take some time for them to round up their stock and to make more bad whiskey. His hope was they'd gone back to wherever they came from to do that.

Midmorning, Maria delivered the two girls freshly scrubbed and dressed in cotton blouses and colorful full skirts. They looked ready to ride.

"They are still very nervous and hardly say a word," she said privately to him.

"After what they have been through," he said, "so would I."

"I heard what that one filthy Comanche did to that Bartlett girl on the stage. He should have it cut off at his belly." Maria's eyes narrowed to slits and the corners of her full mouth turned downward. "You are a good man to do such a thing. If one of my girls were their prisoner, I would hire you to get her back from those savages."

"I would help you," he said, pressing some coins in her hand for the clothing. Though it was used, it was decent and the two looked like white women again. Maybe when their hair grew out and they had some time, they would find some lost pride. They both looked very rejected, waiting for his next order.

"Time to ride," he announced, and led them outside

the cantina. At the rack he unhitched the bay that the mayor had given him.

"Laura Beth, this is your pony."

She stepped forward and he helped her in the saddle. Then he adjusted the stirrups for length. Her feet in sandals, she watched him the entire time, then stuck them in the wooden stirrups.

"Where will we go now?" she asked.

"Santa Fe. Find a train or stage going east."

"How far is that?"

"A very long day's ride. Maybe two." He looked up into the bright sun to see her. "Can you ride that far?"

"I could ride to hell and back with you," she said softly, and then looked away, almost as if she had regretted her strong words. He patted her on the leg and turned his attention to the frailer-looking of the pair.

"Myra, you're next. This roan's yours," he announced.

"I recognize him." She frowned, and then her eyes opened wide at her discovery. "He's from my father's ranch, isn't he?"

"Sure is. I brought him from Texas out here for you to ride home on." He felt elated that she recalled the animal.

"Oh, how wonderful," she gushed as she petted and hugged his face. "They called him Red Apple."

"Sure did," he said, recalling the name. Horses never came when he called them, so he seldom named his. The better and the worse ones all had titles, some he called cuss words, the rest were named by their past owner's name, color, or characteristics.

A memory of home for her, the red roan horse had brought the first sign of life to her that he'd seen so far. The two had a long way to go before they behaved like normal white women again, but he had seen a spark in Myra's eyes.

He swung up on the buckskin and saluted Elandro on the porch. "*Gracias, amigo.* I'll be by again someday."

"I hope it is for fun and good times. Not such serious business."

"We shall have some fun," he agreed. Then he waved to some of the others assembled to see them off before he wheeled the horse around. "Ladies, this way."

The main wagon road, the Camino Real to Santa Fe, was an ancient pathway, hacked out of hillsides dotted with junipers. Used by cumbersome, squeaky oxcarts and burro trains for two centuries, it followed the creek until it joined the rushing Rio Grande, which swept southward through more small villages like Cordova.

They drew the barks and growls of cur dogs that rushed out from small homesteads along the way, the blinking stares of women looking up from hoeing in the small irrigated fields. The three of them rode under the tamaracks and cottonwoods, enjoying the reprieve from the warm sun. Not much had been said between them as they crossed through the land of farmers and into the desert again, not far from the river.

The next stretch of the King's Highway was over a mountain range. The trail grew steep in places, but the horses were shod and travel went uneventfully. Again the tracks went downhill and led them beside the Rio Grande's surging stream. He watered the horses while the two women went off and relieved themselves in the bushes. Then they rested in the grove of trees.

He heard riders coming.

"Mount up, we may have to run for it," he said, helping Myra onto the roan. Laura was already on her horse. He swung on the buckskin and drew the Spencer out of the scabbard under his knee.

"Ride on fast," he shouted to them. "I will catch up with you. The next village is several miles south. I'll be along as soon as I see who it is."

He slapped the closest horse on the rump to urge them

out of there. No time to waste. If it wasn't Comanche or Updikes coming, he'd catch up with them.

"Ride!" he shouted, and they raced off to the south.

The .50-caliber repeater was not a long-range weapon, but he was satisfied it was more effective than the .44 Winchester he traded to the Comanches. Both rifles lacked the range of a good Sharps or Hawkins muzzle loader, something he wanted desperately in his hands as he viewed the leather-clad forms of three Updikes at the top of the hill, riding hard in his direction.

The girls had a quarter mile head start or better, and their horses had not been pushed hard so far. They should outdistance the Updikes regardless of whether he survived stopping them or not. He could see the dust of their ponies far down the sage brush flat. Surely someone would protect them in the next village until he got there.

He flipped up the rear sight of the rifle. Allowing plenty of range, he eased his breath and squeezed off the trigger at the oncoming riders. His shot split them up. One was racing east and wide, the other two were firing their pistols. He could see the gun smoke and then heard the reports, but they might as well have thrown rocks at the range.

He would have to stay and fight them and hope that none got by him and then caught up with the girls. He backed into the cottonwoods to take his stand with the river behind him; a giant log presented good cover for him. His buckskin horse hurriedly picketed in the trees, he took the saddlebags that contained cartridge tubes for the Spencer and some jerky.

It might be a long afternoon, listening to the rush of the river. Two of the Updikes had taken to the tree cover a quarter mile upstream and he couldn't see to shoot at them. The other was out of sight, his half-broken horse fleeing at the first shot. Slocum's main concern was the pair he could hear cussing him out.

"We aim to get you, Slocum, you no good bastard, and

nail your worthless hide to the shithouse wall!''

''You're done messing with us Updikes.''

He thought he saw one of their hats through the foliage. He used the log to steady the rifle and took aim. The loud report hurt his ears and smoke from the muzzle burned his eyes. There was no more yakking from them. Whether his shot found a mark or was close he could only guess. The best part was it silenced them.

He deliberately ejected the smoking cartridge and listened for the wind rustling the leaves and the flowing river. If they tried to rush him, he had his two Colts, one in his holster and the other in his boot. Both were .31 caliber. Some folks called them toys, but at close range he had found them more accurate and effective than the larger-caliber cap and ball revolvers.

No sounds from the Updikes. It might be a long afternoon. He chewed off a hung of jerky and settled in behind his log. He had lots of time. While he didn't consider the Updikes as brazen killers, they were back-shooters and opportunists. They were vengeful enough that they'd try to pay him back for the havoc he had caused them, or die trying.

When nightfall finally came, he intended to end this standoff. No need to risk getting shot in the daylight. Maybe the other one on the runaway horse would come back by then. Thank goodness for the stiff breeze that swept his face, cooling the hot air.

Hatless, he rose and checked carefully for any sign of them. Then he slipped with the rifle to the river end of the log and fired three snap shots in their direction. No reply, he crept back up to the center; that should warn them not to get too close. He gnawed on the jerky and wondered how his wards were making out. They would be safer in the next village than with him at the moment. He'd catch up with them. Stupid whiskey peddlers, anyway.

An hour passed. Slocum had sat on his butt long

enough. The Updikes had not returned a single shot since his volley of rifle shots. He was gaining nothing sitting there, and the Updikes could be sneaking up Indian-style on him. But somehow he considered them cowards unless they had a definite advantage.

He surveyed the grove and saw nothing. The extra Colt jammed in his waistband, Spencer in his hands, he slipped over the log and sought cover behind the next large tree trunk. His movements were deliberate and he kept in mind that the three might have moved closer to his position.

A magpie cawed in the branches overhead. He wished he could silence all the sounds of the river, wind and everything, but there was no way. Nothing in sight, he worked his way through the grove tree by tree.

Where were their horses? He should see them. Had they out tricked him? He ran to the last cottonwood and studied the sage- and juniper-studded hillside. They had fled or, worse, had gone around him.

''Aw, hell!'' he swore aloud as he closed his eyes and shook his head at the realization that they had outsmarted him. Grimly he studied their tracks in the sand. They'd gone back, no doubt found a wash, circled around, and outdone him. He hurried for his horse. Hellfire, he had underestimated them—they didn't want his hide half as bad as they wanted the women. And they had a good hour's head start on him, perhaps more.

The girls were well mounted but defenseless. He slung his saddlebags over the horn, jammed the rifle in the scabbard, and redid the cinch. Then he mounted, sending the buckskin racing southward. Damn, he'd been outdone by the Updikes and the girls might be the ones to pay.

6

"No, señor, there have been no girls like you ask about come by here today," the man said, holding his hand up to shade him from the sun.

Slocum slapped the saddle horn. How had he been so stupid? They'd doubled back on him and he'd miss seeing their tracks. He needed to ride back and find where the Updikes had taken off with the girls. In his haste he had overlooked their tracks and movement in the sandy road bed.

"You're sure?" he asked, hoping the man might have missed seeing them pass by.

"My children, they play all day out here and see everything. Have you seen two señoritas today on horseback ride by here?" he asked the dusty urchins playing in the sand.

"No," came the chorus.

"Three men in buckskin clothing, like I wear. Did they ride by?" Slocum asked them.

Their heads shook no.

"I am sorry, señor, but there has not been much traffic today. Water your fine horse at my tank and rest in the shade of my yard. He is very lathered. My oldest son, Guero, will cool him out for you so he does not become stiff."

"A fine idea," Slocum agreed.

"I have some wine and maybe you would eat some of my Juanita's food?" the man asked as the anxious boy took the heavily breathing horse by the reins and began to lead him.

"I'd better take some time for the horse's sake. Thanks for your hospitality."

"It is nothing. Come and sit in the shade."

The man showed him to a bench in the shade of the mesquites. Then he called to his wife that he needed some wine and food. Located on the road, this family must offer such services to other travelers, Slocum decided as he tried to imagine the place the Updikes could have split off the road and where they had gone with the girls.

No matter, he would find them.

"You come from the mountains?" his host asked.

"Cordova. I ransomed two young women from the Comanches."

"Aye, that is dangerous business, señor. I hope I never see another Comanche again." He shook his head ruefully.

"You speak of Comanches?" the woman asked quietly as she came with a tray of food and a bottle of wine.

"They came to trade at Cordova," her man said, nodding to her.

"It is dangerous business to trade with them, señor. They are the worst. Like a dog that will bite the hand that feeds them." She closed her eyes and shook her head in disapproval as she set the tray beside him. "They are the devil's workers here on earth." She straightened. "Is it enough, señor?" Indicating the food, she waited for his reply.

"Plenty, *gracias*." He looked over the bowl of red chilies and the stack of corn tortillas and nodded his approval. His host poured him wine in a pottery cup.

"What happened to the women? Comanches take them?" he asked quietly as he looked around to be certain none were in hearing range.

"No, they were taken by some evil white men that outsmarted me."

"What will you do?"

"Find their tracks and get them back."

"God be with you. Is the wine all right?"

"Very good." He toasted his host.

Full of the spicy food and settled, Slocum knew he must ride north, find the tracks, and go after the men and girls. His buckskin horse was cooled out and resting in the shade. He paid his host and the boy, then he tightened the cinch. He swung up, saluted the shouting children and the smiling woman in the doorway.

Then he set the buckskin in a trot and rose in the stirrups. He had miles to cover. Riding wide of the road in the loose sand that surrounded the low-growing sage and bunch grass, he sought some sign of where they had taken the girls from the road.

Maybe the two girls had escaped and ridden cross-country. He looked to the distant snowcapped peaks in the east and shook his head. Such a vast land and no clues to their direction.

He reached a crossing on the Rio Grande in late afternoon. Before a small cantina in the village, he reined up his horse, hitched him, and went inside. The sour-smelling interior assailed his nose, while a few candles gave a shaky light in the cavernous atmosphere.

"Señor? What can I do for you?" a short man behind the crude bar asked.

"Did some men in buckskin and two women cross the river here today."

"Miguel," the man called to a customer seated at a table.

"Did you see anyone make the crossing?"

"Gringos?" the man asked, turning to looking at him and Slocum.

"Yes. In buckskins."

"*Sí*, perhaps three hours ago." The man turned back to his conversation with the others at his table.

"*Gracias,*" Slocum said, tossing the bartender a quarter and pitching one to the surprised man at the table.

The man rose and bowed, then he pointed. "They went north. There were five of them."

"I appreciate the information," Slocum said, and ducked outside.

Mounted on his horse, he felt certain for the first time that he knew the direction they had taken and that both girls were their prisoners. He crossed the river at the shoal. Over knee deep on his mount, he soon splashed up the far side. North of this ford, he knew the Rio Grande cut through a half-mile-deep gorge for miles with few places to cross it.

Unless they intended to fool him and cut back at some-place upstream, they were headed into the high country. The land was unfamiliar to him; he knew it only from others' descriptions—a place of year-round snow-capped mountain ranges, alpine meadows, elk, mule deer, bear, along with hostile Utes and some northern Apaches driven from the plains by their enemies, the Comanches.

Under the late evening sun, he studied to the far-off red-tinted snow-topped Rockies. Somewhere up there, the Updikes had a den like old bears. That was where they felt safe and would take the women. No doubt some kind of a fortress. He trotted the buckskin. The loose sand in the road left few clear tracks and told him little except that he was on their trail.

At a water hole, he recognized in the mud the shoeprint of the roan that he had reset. He also noted two other distinct hoof tracks. Satisfied he was only a few hours behind them, he pushed on.

At dark he made camp without a fire in a grove of junipers. His gaze on the vast land around him, he unsaddled his buckskin, hobbled him, and then spread a blanket on the ground. By dawn he intended to be moving again. His greatest concern was the Updikes might discover his trailing them. He wanted his arrival to be a big surprise and have the advantage.

They had to know he was on their trail, he finally decided as he rolled up in his blankets. On his side, he studied the star-studded sky, listened to the mournful coyotes howling, and wondered how his wards fared. A timber wolf's throaty voice cut the night. He shut his eyes to the notion of their problems with their kidnappers and soon slept.

He awoke. It was still night. Half awake, he heard a horse snort nearby. The buckskin nickered in return. He pushed the blankets aside and the night's coolness swept his face as he tried to see around the dark juniper forms. Colt in his hand, he surged to his feet. Who was out there?

How many were there?

"Slocum?"

"That you, Laura Beth?" he asked, squinting to better see her.

"Yes, oh, thank God," she cried, and rushed into his arms. Hugging him, he wondered if she had been followed by the Updikes. He tried to see past her, but nothing else showed in the pearl light that flooded the grassland beyond them.

"How did you escape?" he asked, holding her trembling form.

"I lived with Comanches for many months. These men were not that smart." She cuddled closer to him. "Oh, thank God, I found you."

"Did they follow you?" he asked, holstering his revolver.

"I don't think so. They acted real anxious to get to their place in Colorado."

"How is Myra?"

"She is still in shock." She nested her face on his chest. "I tried to get her to run away with me. There was not much time. She acted as if she never heard me. So I got on her roan bareback and left when the men were busy. A good thing he knew your horse and nickered to him, or I would have ridden right by you."

"How far ahead are they?"

"I took the roan shortly after dark and rode him hard until I was sure there was no one on my back trail. Then I trotted him, seems like forever."

"Maybe ten miles ahead," he guessed out loud.

"I don't know. Hold me, Slocum." She wrapped her arms around him and pressed her body to his. "I am so glad to be here, I can hardly believe my good fortune."

He looked down into her face and then lowered his lips. Her hunger for his affection became a flash fire, and her arms quickly encircled his neck. Her sun-cracked lips were soon wet and seeking more of him.

Out of breath, they finally sought some relief. Standing so tight to him, her hard breasts bore holes in him. He wondered if she wished to continue.

"I need you," she whispered, and pulled his face down to hers for more.

The fire began to rise in his brain. His hand sought her teardrop-shaped breast, and she sighed at his touch. Then, to help him, she undid her blouse and pressed his hand to her bare breast. His mind swirling, he massaged her nipples until they turned rock hard. Flush with excitement, she wiggled down the skirt from her hips. He toed off his boots and dropped the gun belt as he admired her slender hips and smooth stomach in pearly starlight.

His fingers fumbled with his own shirt buttons, and

soon discarded the garment. Unbuttoning freed the growing pressure inside his pants. He stripped his britches off and the cool night air rushed over his bare skin as he swallowed hard. Before him stood a lovely, mature woman. She stepped in close; her fist encircled his manhood as if testing it, then she stood on her toes and kissed him.

"Be gentle, I am still sore." Her shoulders shook and then her breasts trembled. Impulsively she hugged them.

"I will," he promised as they both knelt down on his blankets. Soon they lay side by side, and he drew the cover over them for warmth.

She pulled him on top of her and spread her slender legs apart for him. Over her, he let her guide his root inside her slowly, despite his growing need to be in her. Soon he was halfway in her and she released her hold. His hips began to move, and she raised her butt to meet him as he drove deeper. Their actions began to quicken as he sought her fiery volcano. Her sharp cries of pleasure urged him inward deeper and deeper.

His breath raged through his nose as he pumped her harder and harder. The convulsive wave of muscles inside her grew tighter and tighter. Her eyes were squeezed shut and the strain of her effort showed even in her slender jaw.

Her mouth flew open, she cried out loud, then in a faint sank away under him. He eased his way until she again began to arouse to his actions. Soon she became the fiery receptor to his efforts. Her legs locked around him, she hunched herself to him with all her might—she wanted him to the hilt. Waves of her contractions pulled on his root until they drove him home, and then the final fireworks burst across the ceiling of her cavern.

They lay in a heap together and slept.

7

"There must be a hundred of them," Laura explained as the herd of elk cows and calves raised their heads. The curious young ones sniffed the air and then shook their heads at the obvious new odor of man and horse. Several cows acted skeptical and ready to flee at a moment's notice. A few trotted downwind and then tested the air, as if uncertain.

Earlier in the day he had shot a yearling mule deer for their food supply. The notion of elk steaks made his mouth water, but for him to kill one would be a waste of a lot of meat. They'd use most of the small deer before it spoiled.

"They are huge, aren't they?" she asked as she pushed the roan forward with the heels of her sandals.

"Big animals. They say they once roamed the plains with the buffalo."

"What happened to them?" she asked.

"Shot out, and the rest took refuge in the highest mountains up here."

"I saw an elkskin jacket," she said. Excitement sparkled in her eyes. "They traded for it. Oh, it was soft and heavy too."

"They make good ones," he agreed, and searched the timber line above them for any sign of human life. He didn't need to ride into an Updike trap. Somewhere they would lay one for him. They had the choice of time and place. He had to be ready.

He had had an elkskin jacket once. It was snow-white and had long fringe on the sleeves. A Sioux woman made it for him. He could not forget the turn of her long hip when she walked naked around the lodge to tease him. One-Who-Runs was her name.

He bought her from the Crows. Three young bucks rode into his camp, leading her, hands tied together and feet bound under the small animal's belly. She rode with her head high, like a queen, despite her captive state.

"Big man, you want her?" the oldest of the boys asked.

"How much?"

"Two buffalo hides and some gunpowder."

She sat straight-backed on the pony. Her slender face was the color of red sandstone and looked chiseled by an artist. Dark eyes filled with anger, he wondered if during their first night together she might slip a sharp knife between his ribs.

In typical Indian fashion, as if they had all the time in the world, the three bucks squatted at his fire and ate some of the deer ribs he had cooked, flinging the bones aside after sucking them dry. Their mouths shined with deer grease on them as they grinned knowingly at each other, waiting for his reply.

"Has she been with men?" he asked.

They looked at each other foolishly and then shared a secret without words.

"She told us she was a virgin," the eldest said, and flung another bone aside. "That was yesterday." They giggled at his words.

"What can I do with her?" Slocum asked, acting disinterested.

"Whatever you like." He elbowed the one on the right between his next bites on the meaty rib. They laughed at the notion and nodded. *Do whatever you like with her.*

"Did it take all three of you to hold her down?"

The youngest of the crew glanced at the girl on horseback as if considering her strength, then he looked back at Slocum and nodded.

"We don't care what you do to her," the eldest said. "Kill her if you like, she is only a dog-eating Sioux." Then he found another rib in the pot to suit him.

"Slocum, when will we be in Colorado?" Laura asked, breaking into his thoughts.

"Somewhere north of here. I doubt there're any markers to show the way."

"There's a town called Injun Springs, where those Updikes intended to get supplies."

"Never heard of it. But this is all new country to me."

"Gorgeous, isn't it?" she asked over her shoulder as she rode ahead of him.

"Pretty as any you'll ever see," he said as he studied the high peaks shining like gray gun-barrel material and capped with snow.

"Won't it be nice to find an unclaimed valley and build a ranch somewhere up here?" she asked.

"Be real nice if the circumstances were different."

"Oh, I know. But—" She shrugged as if she felt she had been too outspoken about such a thing.

She didn't know that wanted posters for him decorated many a storefront window across the west. Nor did she even suspect that a rich man in Fort Scott, Kansas, kept the Abbott brothers supplied with cash and expenses in a relentless pursuit of him. But, hell, if it wasn't them, then the man would hire someone else, perhaps more astute at bounty hunting than those two brothers. Still, he never knew when a reward-hungry gun toter would try to collect the sum on his head.

A sow bear reared up on the trail before her and roared. The roan horse, shocked by the awesome stinking creature before him, whirled and plunged off the hillside, unseating Laura. Savagely snarling, with saliva dripping from her fangs, she charged the downed Laura.

"Curl in a ball!" he screamed, dismounting to go to her rescue. He jerked the Spencer free a second before the buckskin panicked and fled up the steep face of the mountain.

His first shot was high and creased the bear's back, causing it to snap at its own sides as it stood over Laura Beth. He levered a second shot in the chamber on the move, yelling at the top of his lungs to distract the bear away for her.

A savage paw from the sow rolled Laura Beth over, tearing her blouse and coming up with shreds of material stuck to its blood-covered claws. His second shot struck behind her front legs. The bullet drew a puff of dust, and the sow whirled with a savage growl and charged him. The next bullet from his rifle went through her brain, but she was on him by then.

Slammed down on the rocks by her hurling charge, the air gone from his lungs, Slocum strained to breathe. The terrific dead odor of the animal's breath in his face, he fought to draw his Colt. Her sharp teeth sunk into his head as he drove the muzzle of the handgun into her throat and fired.

Her teeth snapped shut as they slipped off his skull, and she began to strangle as her sticky red blood began to pour out of the gunshot wound above him. He cocked the pistol and fired again into the thick fur under her chin.

She made another savage snap, as if straining to find what enemy caused her such pain. Her hind paws mashing his legs and pinning him in place, he tried without success, to roll out from under her. He was pinned in place, and the pain in his leg shot like lightning into his head. Over him he could see her strain to open her bloody mouth and try to catch her breath. Then she dropped back on her butt, putting more weight on his legs and causing him to cry out. *Die, damn you!*

Gurgling on her own blood, she collapsed in a thud on top of him. His face smothered in her bloody fur, the excruciating weight of her form pressing down, he could hardly get his breath.

"Slocum? Slocum, are you alive?" Laura Beth cried on the ground beside him.

"Get a horse and pull her off me," he managed to say. "Hurry, girl. I can hardly breathe."

"Don't give up. They've run off," she said. "I'll find a horse. Slocum, I'll hurry."

The filthy fur taste in his nose and mouth, he fought for his breath as he listened to Laura's footfall as she ran away. Heavier and heavier the dying bear pressed down on him. He tried to get his hands and arms under the sow's chest to raise her, but straining as hard he could, he still remained pinned down. The throes of death made the involuntary muscles of the animal jerk and ground him more. Then she pissed all over him.

He'd known someday that he'd die somewhere, but he never figured it would be crushed to death by a pissy stinking bear. His breathing became more desperate as the seconds fled by. How far had the buckskin gelding gone? No telling, maybe Colorado. The animal had panicked at the bear's attack. He'd charged up the face of the mountain, shedding loose talus rock with each hop.

A few years before, high in the Rockies near Wagon Gap, Colorado, he'd seen a man ripped apart by a charging grizzly and three other men shooting it full of holes at the same time. The poor gold seeker died a horrible death.

Slocum couldn't get his breath, his chest so crushed by the weight of the corpse on top of him. Lucky it was only a black bear. A grizzly would have finished both him and Laura. This one would simply smother him to death. His vision dimmed, and he knew unless he found some air soon, he'd soon die.

"You still breathing? Slocum, talk to me. I ain't never done this before. I have the roan, my God, she hates this bear. Whoa. Whoa.

"Slocum, can you hear me?" she cried out.

He couldn't manage to get a word out.

"Whoa, you stupid horse." He could hear her feet sliding in the gravel as she fought with the animal. "Damn you, horse, we've got to get him out. We may be too late now."

He must have passed out, for when he awoke, she was close by, talking to him. "I got that damn horse tied down the trail and I'm putting a rope on the bear's leg. Damn! She stinks real bad! Oh, God help me." She prayed out loud. "You helped me escape them damn raping Comanches. Please help me save this man.

"God, he's the first real man I ever had, don't let me lose him." Then sounds of her sandals running back uphill on the gravel. *Hurry, girl, I'm so light-headed now!* Faintly, he could hear her arguing with the horse and then bringing him back.

"Whoa! Wait till I get the rope on the horn. Whoa! There, now pull! Dammit, pull, horse! Hell, we've got to get that damn bear off him. Pull! Pull, damn you." He felt the bear start to move, but nothing happened.

"He can't pull it off you!" she cried, more desperate than before. "I've got to find the buckskin to help pull her off. Slocum, stay alive! Where is that yellow horse?"

When he awoke, he was lying naked on the bearskin rug in her lodge. He could see that she planned some form of mischief—it was written on her face since she had returned to the tepee. One-Who-Runs quickly removed the leather dress over her head, then she tossed her fur-wrapped braids back as she stood above him. Her firm, pointed brown breasts shook as she stepped over him and deliberately she lowered herself over his hips.

"I will ride you like a horse," she said slyly.

"Perhaps you will be thrown," he said as she reached between her legs to insert his stiffening root.

"Not from such a stick." She shook her head in disbelief, and then the ermine wraps on her thick braids swung around her smooth shoulders and dangled in his face.

Don't crush me, One-Who-Runs. I can't breathe!

8

"Thank God!" Laura gushed in his face as she knelt on her hands and knees over him. "Slocum, talk to me. I thought I'd never get that bear off you. It took both horses. Talk to me, please. Oh, be alive."

"Butcher the bear," he gasped. Each shallow breath he managed to get out knifed deep inside his lungs. He couldn't feel his feet and wondered what other damage the bear had possibly done to him. "We'll need all of it to survive up here."

"I helped butcher a hog once."

He nodded as he carefully felt his upper body with his right hand. Every rib must be crushed. He closed his eyes to the sun's glare. Excruciating pain raged through his body.

"Can you get up?" she asked. "I can help."

52

"I don't think so. Maybe later." He fought to stay conscious.

"I just can't leave you here on this hillside," she pleaded.

"Put a blanket on me," he said. "Butcher the bear before it's too dark to see."

"I'll butcher the damn bear!" She pushed herself off her knees to stand upright. "First, I'll get you a blanket. You're hurt worse than you're letting on to me. Slocum, damn your soul, don't you dare die on me."

He recalled passing out, then coming around in the darkness. The night's coolness had settled in. He tried to sit up, but the sharp knives of pain kept him flat on his back flat atop the rocky ground. A poor place to die; worse than that, it was a poor place to linger and then die. He could smell wood smoke. Obviously Laura Beth had a fire going. Good, she had some survival sense. He hadn't planned on being out on the trail overnight, so they had no camping gear. The aching in his hip ran down his lower back and into his numb legs. The lack of feeling in his lower body concerned him more than anything else. Being this helpless left him at the mercy of man and beast.

He could send her back on horseback for help and keep one Colt for himself for protection. If she didn't make it back, he could end his own life. He needed to do that first light. Send her for help. Back at the Rio Grande crossing she should be able to hire a rig to move him in. Maybe in a few days he would be able to stand a wagon ride. He closed his eyes to the thunder inside his skull.

"Slocum?" she asked softly. "I brought you some water in the canteen. I've butchered that stinking bear. I'm cooking some if you can eat. Damn, I stink like guts. There's a creek west of here. I filled the canteen there, but had no time to wash."

"You did good," he managed as she lifted his head up and spilled the water on his mouth. Some got into his mouth, the rest ran down his chin and soaked his shirt. He swallowed hard. It was cool.

"You're hurt bad, aren't you?"

"Couple of days I'll be like new." Then he chocked on the water and coughed until tears welled in his eyes. The strain hurt his ribs worse than before.

Her cool palm swept his forehead to push his hair back, and then she eased him down when the spell passed. "Wish I could do more for you."

"I'll be better come first light."

"How?" she asked. He could see her shaking her head in distress as she straightened back on her knees. A profusion of stars sparkled over them and formed a halo around her face.

His breath cut to the quick by his crushed rib cage, his vision of the sky swirled, and then he fainted away, not waking until long past dawn.

"I want to get you in some shade," she said, discovering him awake.

"Won't make no difference. I'm getting up."

"How?" She began to laugh out loud. Her hands were orange with dried blood, the new blouse was torn open in the back, and her skirt was filthy with dust, stained, and ripped. She broke into tears that ran down her dirt-powdered face. He wanted to reach out and comfort her, but there was no way.

"Laura," he said finally, eaten up by her sorrow and despair. "Help me sit up."

"Can you do it?" she asked, quickly reaching under his armpits and helping him to rise.

Out of breath, beads of perspiration streaming down his cheeks, he tried to minimize the hurting in his chest and back. Dizzy, he wondered where his strength had gone.

"I hung up that stinking bear hide with some lariat ropes over there by that cedar tree. It's not much shelter and looks damn crude, but it will shade you if we can get you over there. Trunk of that tree will make a chair back for you. Those cuts on your head from the bear's bites need to be cleaned. You're a mess.''

''I'll get on my knees first,'' he said as she had him sitting up. The facts he faced were he was out of strength and thirty feet from shade.

''Oh.'' She struggled, lifting until he was kneeling. Both of them breathless, they rested. Her face buried in his neck, tears ran down her face.

''I'd better crawl,'' he said.

''I'm sorry I'm not any stronger,'' she apologized.

''Not your fault. We're going to whip this,'' he said, dropping to all fours and then letting the chills of his pain subside in his jaw before he dared to move.

One hand forward, he lifted his right knee, sending lightning up his spine. He tried to disregard the pain and crawled on his elbows off the bank. He moved, one small wiggle at a time. She ran and got the blankets, and quickly spread them out under the bearskin roof.

''You going to make it?'' she asked, coming out to face him.

He never looked up, his breath so short he thought he would black out any minute. Dodging around the low, brittle sage clumps that filled his nose with the pungent sweet spice made the route even longer. Each gasp for air produced a deep knife that ripped him inside from his belt to throat.

His eyes squeezed shut. He rested, lost in the whirlpool of hurt and confusing weakness. Then, like a determined tortoise, he strove for his den one deliberate move at a time. At last he managed to make the shade, and collapsed onto the blanket, listening to the buzzing fly in his ear.

''Slocum,'' she hissed in his ear, fussing over him as he lay facedown. ''There's two Indians coming.''

''Indians?'' He wondered who they were and how far away they were. ''Get me sitting up to the tree.''

''What good is that going to do?'' She frowned, peeved at his request.

"Help me. Where are my guns?"

"Right here with the saddles. This is going to kill you," she said, exasperated, as they both struggled to turn him and to move him the few precious feet until he sat with his back to the juniper. Waves of deep pain coursed his body, and he feared he would pass out again.

"Better than them killing us," he said with a deep sigh.

"I'm not sure. I could probably whip them myself." She glanced to the west and then drew her mouth in a tight, pensive line.

"Get me the Colt," he said, trying to make out the two riders.

One of them wore a silk opera hat and a velvet-trimmed black coat coated in dust. His obvious Indian origin was the chiseled dark face and wrapped braids that hung to his saddle horn. The other rider was bare-headed, big as a red bear, and carried a white parasol for shade. An enormous quill vest encompassed his barrel chest, his only clothing other than a breechclout, and his thick brown legs were bare in the stirrups to his moccasins.

"Who are they?" she asked in a whisper.

"Strange." He shook his head at the sight of the weirdly dressed pair. "Keep an eye on our horses. Those nags they ride ain't much. They may try to steal ours."

"I will. Oh, no, they've seen us. They're coming from the trail."

"I can see them."

"You look bad. What'll I do if you pass out?"

"Kill them."

"Oh!" she gasped, and her shoulders shook with a shudder.

The tall one stepped down. He handed the reins of his ewe-necked horse to his traveling partner and then started forward. He stopped a few feet from the shelter and raised his right hand in the peace sign.

"How," he said, nodding as he appraised the green hide. "Kill great bear?"

"Who are you?" Slocum asked. His vision hazy, he wondered why his legs were still too numb to have feeling in them as he studied the strangely dressed buck before him. Where in God's name had he found such an outfit?

"Me Lone Eagle, him Barcelona Bill." He gave a toss toward his partner.

"Lone Eagle. Barcelona Bill? What kind of Indians are you?"

"No tribe. All die. What is your tribe?" The man squatted at the edge of the shade and looked at Slocum critically. His partner, the big one, sat his paint, not making a move.

"No tribe. Slocum's my name."

Eagle nodded that he heard him. "That bear hurt you?"

"Some."

"There is a place near here where Indians heal."

"No thanks." Slocum shook his head.

Laura cleared her throat to get his attention, standing above him. "Maybe they would help me move you there?" she asked him softly.

"What do you want?" Slocum asked, ignoring her request.

"A bearskin." Eagle indicated it.

"Not for sale."

"We could move you to the place that heals. There are some empty lodges there."

The world began to spin. The Colt slipped from his fingers and he felt as if he had been pitched off into a deep black chasm by the two Indians and kept falling into the inky darkness.

Slocum awoke in the shade. He blinked his eyes as Laura walked beside, holding the parasol over him. The travois poles bearing him sizzled along in the dirt. Despite the discomfort on an occasional bump over a rock, the sling ride was not bad.

"You trade them the hide?" he demanded.

"Yes," she said under her breath as she hurried to keep

up and shade him at the same time. "They say we'll be to this healing place by dark."

"Once they get us away from the road, they'll probably cut our throats and steal everything," he hissed at her. There was nothing he could do either. He closed his eyes to the pain and discomfort of the bumps. No matter what he wanted to do, in this condition he was their prisoner.

"It's going to work. You'll see," she said with resolve. "They think I'm your wife."

"Good."

"Why?"

"Then they won't mess with you."

"Sure."

Lady Luck had saved him before, maybe she would this time too. His fate was in the hands of a girl and two no-tribe Indians. He was being dragged to God knew where. *Jim Ed, I've not only lost your daughter, I may have lost my life too. Some mess I've got myself in.*

9

A gagging odor awoke him. Hellfire and brimstone was all he could think of. He discovered he was lying on a bed beneath a brush arbor. Not a real bedstead, but one made of pine boughs set in a log frame. But where was that terrible smell coming from? Had someone left the gates of hell open? Without rising, he could see various lodges around them. Where was Laura? Had those two misfits raped and killed her?

He was in an Indian camp. He'd noticed a squaw in fringed buckskin go by carrying a pot under her arm. There were children in the camp, he could hear their yelling and playing. What did that opera-hatted one mean by *no tribe*? About then, he heard, to his relief, Laura talking a hundred miles an hour and someone jabbering some guttural Indian back at her.

"Slocum, this is Heals-Good," she announced. "Eagle

59

says she is a great healer among the mountain tribes.''

The woman had one distracting blind eye. Her other one scrutinized him like a buzzard looking at a pile of fresh guts. Like a predator she pounced on his foot and began to twist off his boot without much concern for the discomfort her effort caused him, though he felt nothing except the tug. She peeled his sock away and threw it down.

''Don't let the stray dogs get my boots and socks,'' he said to Laura, not taking his eye off the woman. He had not felt a thing except for some sharpness in his waist when she jerked it off, a fact that niggled him as she turned his leg to the left and right. Then she dropped it on the blanket and did the same exercise to the other one. Satisfied that Laura had gathered his footgear together, he wondered what this one-eyed quack would do next.

She undid his pants and then pulled them off in none too gentle a fashion. He felt very obvious as she handed them to Laura. Then she bent his knee toward his body and looked at him for an answer. Could he do that?

''No.'' He shook his head.

''What's the matter with your legs?'' Laura asked, discovering his problem.

''Ask her. They don't work,'' he said, watching the woman as she went around the bed to try the other one.

''Eagle says she is a very good doctor,'' Laura said to reassure him of her skills. ''There was a woman like her with the Comanches that cured many.''

Heals-Good raised his other leg carefully and then bent it at the knee, searching him for an answer again. Did she want to know if it hurt?

''No.'' He shook his head, unable to do a thing with his lower body.

She visibly pinched the white skin and then looked for his reply. When he shook his head, she nodded and motioned for Laura to come over and help her. She undid his shirt, and they held him up to take it off. He flinched at the pain that shot through him when they raised his arms to remove it.

A cool wind swept over his bare skin as they lowered him back down. The effort had totally exhausted him. Next they rolled him over on his stomach. His breath grew short and he closed his eyes as her callused hands ran over his back. She was searching for something there. Despite his skepticism, he was impressed by her thoroughness. Then her thumb found something along his spine and he tried to muffle the sharp cry of pain that came from his mouth.

The waves of agony finally passed and he floated in and out of consciousness. The woman was gone when he came around again. Strain-faced, Laura knelt beside him.

"Can you hear me, Slocum? She didn't mean to hurt you."

"I know," he managed to say. "Where did she go?"

"To do something or get something. I don't know."

"Where is Lone Eagle? He steal my guns and horses?" he asked, lying on his stomach in discomfort.

"No, he needed a deer's brains to tan the bear hide I gave him."

"So you gave him my rifle and horse?"

"Don't be so upset," she said. "Barcelona Bill is still here. For heaven's sake, they helped me get you here!"

He closed his eyes. The girl was blinded by those two misfits' smooth talking. But there was nothing he could do in his condition.

"Are you warm enough?" she asked. "Maybe I can find another cover."

"I'm warm enough. But I can hardly breathe this way."

"I think she's bringing some help."

"What?"

"I'm not sure, but she's rounded up all the women in camp and I think she has a stretcher."

Heals-Good took charge, and soon he was rolled none

too gently onto a litter. The move hurt him, but he bit down and fought crying out. Laura indicated to them that he needed to be on his back, and the woman agreed. Then she covered his nakedness with a blanket as the four women carried him through the camp on the springy litter.

Not knowing what they would do to him next, he reserved any comment. Children ran alongside, daring peeks at the helpless white man. The fumes of the sulphurous breath became closer. That was the odor that had awakened him. Sulphur! That was the smell. They were at some kind of hot springs that he could hear spewing around them. He knew Indians considered such places as neutral holy grounds.

What would be his fate? He'd probably have his privates boiled off by being lowered into some scalding fountain. A cold chill at the thought of such a fate made him shiver despite the sun and soft blanket covering his nakedness.

Heals-Good uncovered him, then she began giving orders to the buckskin-clad squaws. They raised him to a sitting position, two formed a seat with their arms, and he was taken off the litter. He closed his eyes to the hurt in his torso.

Then he felt them lower him into a pool of hot water that he couldn't feel on his feet or legs, but the heat swept his face and the smell took his breath. His worst fears were happening, they were going to boil him alive, balls and all. His heart stopped. He was sitting on the bottom, and Heals-Good had fastened a leather strap under his arms tied to a bar overhead to keep him from drowning.

Someone else was in the pool. Both men blinked at the discovery of the other. A full-faced Indian was likewise suspended on the overhead pole arrangement that held him him up.

"Who are you?" the Indian demanded. The big man,

no doubt of some authority, looked outraged at the intrusion of a white man in the same pool.

"Slocum. Who the hell are you?"

"Bull Elk, chief of the Utes."

"Well, welcome to hellfire and brimstone, great chief."

"Why are you on my land?" The man tried to rise to show his authority.

"A bear ran over me. I was looking for the Updikes."

"You trade with them?" Dark brows hooded his coal-black pupils as he waited for answer.

"No. They kidnapped a woman from me. I want them dead."

Bull Elk hung in his harness, considering Slocum's words. Deep in thought, he acted interested in the water. Then finally he looked up and agreed. "They sell bad whiskey, poison my people. Cheat them out of their hides and furs. Need to be killed."

"What is wrong with you?"

"Horse fell from mountain."

"This woman Heals-Good is the best?" he asked.

Bull Elk nodded and sulked in silence, as if considering greater things. The strap ate at his armpits, and were it not for the buoyancy of the water holding his weight, the arrangement would be excruciating.

Slocum lost track of time. Near sundown they took him from the steamy pool. Two women waded in and hoisted him out. He thought they were naked, but he was in such a daze, he couldn't tell. Next thing he knew, the cool air was rushing over his body. Relieved at the discovery that he could finally draw a breath of fresh air that wasn't totally sulphur tainted, they dried him. Then the team of women who had carried him to the spring took him back to his bed under the shelter on the stretcher. He found his eyelids too heavy to stay open.

"You've got to eat. She told Lone Eagle you must eat this broth." Laura said, worried.

"He come back?"

"Yes," she said, sounding perturbed that he would ask. She held his head up to spoon in the hot soup. "I have some willow-bark tea to ease the pain when you eat this."

"My leg," he said, "I can feel it."

"What?"

"My right leg is asleep. Rub it." He tried to sit up, excited about the needles and pins that went to his foot. Caught short by the pain in his chest, he squirmed on his back to move the leg. It twisted right and then left a little as Laura rubbed it with her hand.

"No!" Heals-Good ordered, and pulled her away. She stayed the leg and shook her head at him, holding the limb firmly in place.

"She says not to move it," Lone Eagle said, translating, bent over under the roof with the top hat in his hands. "Too soon, you must not use it."

Frowning, Heals-Good issued more sharp orders to the tall, lean man to translate for her.

"She says feeling will only come and go now."

The one-eyed healer mischievously grinned at him as she lifted the cover with one hand. With her index finger she raised his limp root and then let it fall back. Smug-looking, she spoke to Eagle as she replaced the cover over him.

"Heals-Good says soon that too will work."

"Oh, Slocum, you're going to get better!" Laura shouted, and kissed his beard-stubbled face.

He closed his eyes as Lone Eagle stressed what she said, that he must eat the soup and drink the tea. The pins and needles in his improving limb were becoming more distracting. His heart pounded at the woman's success. He hoped she was right about her diagnosis. *Would he recover?* He looked to the sky; somewhere an angel was looking after him. How much could he expect? It wasn't fair to ask her; besides, she was already leaving in a sweep of her stained deerskin dress.

10

On his crutches, he hobbled to his daily bath. By his consideration of the passing moon quarters, they had been at the springs over a month. His ribs had healed enough to allow him to swing his way up the slight incline on the supports to the pool for the several hours of soaking. Heals-Good and another woman called Willow had been working his back with massage after each day in the bath. His left leg was still not responding, and the fact concerned him as he watched them carry away the Ute chief on the litter.

Bull Elk could be heard at times loudly complaining that the healing woman had not done all she could for him. In fact, to save any arguments between him and the man, Heals-Good, had asked him to come to the pool after the chief. Slocum wondered as sat on the log, undressing, if the Ute would ever recover or if his back injuries were permanent. Eagle had warned that the man had a violent temper and his incapacity had made him even angrier than ever.

As he eased himself into the water, Slocum wondered if he would have ended own his life without the care and recovery offered by the one-eyed woman. Her four helpers were widows; sickness or injury of family members had brought them to the hot springs. They helped Heals-Good keep the camp, which nestled in a narrow canyon. A series of natural boiling vats and some hot mud pots spat a brownish, gooey muck. This larger one that he slipped into with some effort by himself was the spillover basin from the source.

Laura's Indians, he called the unlikely pair. Lone Eagle had proved a good hunter for the camp, and with the aid of his powerful partner, Bill, the two had kept everyone in fresh meat without wasting a single bullet. They'd used the buckskin and roan horse for hunting and packing, leading them in each time laden with deer, big-horn sheep, or elk, while their own mounts were recovering some weight, grazing and resting.

He'd learned that Lone Eagle was from the Iowa tribe, and Bill's mother was a Fox, he thought. She lived with those people when he was little. The two men had met each other on the plains as young boys. Both often beaten by the camp elders, they had fled home early. Not members of a tribe, they had lived among half breeds and other outcasts, wandering, not accepted by the other tribes. Bill's first wife died of smallpox. Some trappers had killed Lone Eagle's woman—small details they'd told him around the campfire at night.

Slocum stretched out his right leg under the water as the high sun sought his face. He felt something new. In disbelief he tested and he could wiggle his left leg, even move his toes. The pins and needles were there, as they had when the feeling first started to return to his other leg. He swallowed hard and looked into the sun to give his thanks. Both his legs would work again. The woman had done miracles.

When could he ride again? He needed to find Jim Ed's daughter. What condition would he find her in among those trappers? Still, he needed to recover her and take her back to him in Kansas. He started to get out of the stinking water, but then he settled down again. He could hardly wait to tell Laura the good news. The poor girl had waited on him hand and foot. She'd made herself an elkskin dress from a hide her hunters brought her and sewed him a new deerskin shirt. When he went for his treatment she was making him new britches from some hides that she'd tanned.

When he was satisfied the length of his stay in the water was sufficient, he climbed out. Seated on the flat rock and drying himself, he was joined by Heals-Good. Since the woman knew every part of his body, being naked before her did not bother either of them.

"My leg," he said, and he showed her how he could extend it and twist it back and forth. "I can feel it."

She touched her finger to her lips to quiet him. Then she looked west, toward the chief's encampment. His large tepee poles struck above the junipers. She was telling him that the chief must not learn that he was better. Suspicious as they were, he understood that Bull Elk would think he had stolen all her medicine.

"Should I leave?" he asked, in sign language.

"No." She made signs that he must stay another moon. She squatted on her heels and looked concerned at the Ute's tepee top.

"I will use the crutches." He held them up to show her.

She agreed.

Obviously the chief was not responding to the treatment. It was not his fault, but it could cause a big problem for her and the lot of them.

She placed a hand on his bare leg and then looked down at his rising root. Then she smiled knowingly and shook her head in disapproval as she rose. On her feet, she put her hands on her hips and shoved her small belly forward to stretch her back muscles. Then she wagged her middle finger in his face and shook her head in disapproval.

He understood her. He watched her start off, enjoying the movements of the leather dress. She paused, turned slowly, and shook her head again for his sake. He smiled and held up his hands in defence. She had no worry, he wouldn't consider her then, but it felt damn good to know he might someday.

He dressed, enjoying the birds' chirping and finally feeling more settled about his own recovery. He was going to get well. At last he could make plans to get under way. Then, as he rose and tried his left leg, he recalled the crutches. He tucked them under his arms and began his trip back to their lodge.

Laura looked up at his approach. Setting aside her sewing, she rose and greeted him.

"How was the bath today?"

"Stinking like always," he said.

"I made some tea."

"Good," he said, wishing instead for a few stiff drinks to celebrate his good fortune. He lowered himself onto the Navajo blanket on the bed that she had traded for.

"I wish we could find a case of Arbuckle coffee or real whiskey," he said as she poured tea into the tin can.

"I think that is impossible," she said as she served him the steaming container. "But this stuff is better than that root stuff that Lone Eagle dug up."

"For sure. Listen closely, this is a secret," he said, checking around to be certain they were alone and out of earshot of anyone.

"What?" she asked on her knees before him.

"My other leg is working," he whispered.

"Wonderful!" She threw her arms around his neck and almost threw him down.

"Shush. Bull Elk is not recovering, and he thinks I have all Heals-Good's medicine. For her sake he cannot learn of my recovery."

She paled under the freckled tan that bridged her face. "How can we do that?"

"I need to use the crutches and act as if I am not better. She says I still need more time to heal fully. It is too soon for some important things."

"Important things?" Her brown lashes blinked in question.

His eyes went to his lap and then he smiled for her.

"Yes. It has recovered too?" Laura wondered.

"She said it was too soon, but, yes, it has recovered." In fact, it was back to its old self as he sat there, and the pressure in his pants was making him restless, another reason he felt so elated.

"Thank God," she whispered in his ear, and kissed him, hugging his face to hers. "I am ready when you are." Then, red-faced at her own words, she rose and went back to her sewing project.

"I guess that Eagle and Bill wish to go with us when we leave?" he said, sitting on the edge of the bed.

"When will that be?"

"I'm not sure," he said, blowing the steam off the lip of the tin can and looking down the canyon. "Heals-Good doesn't want me to rush it. That's obvious, and since she has me almost well, I guess we'll stay here awhile longer."

"What about Bull Elk?" she asked under her breath as she strained to push the steel needle through the leather seam of his new pants.

"We shall act no differently."

"The rubdown team is coming. You'd better get undressed," she said as Heals-Good and two more women came up the path.

He removed his moccasins, took his shirt off over his head, and then nodded to his healer.

Pants too, she indicated as he started to lie down on his stomach. He quickly shucked them, but not before her helper, Willow, covered her giggling mouth at the sight of his erection. The other woman whose name he could not pronounce, began to titter too. Without word he rolled onto his back.

She spoke sharply to the two and then they began to massage his legs. They continued to talk and laugh about what he considered his recovered root. Better to be the point of their humor than not work at all.

He felt the woman's hands for the first time as Willow worked on his left leg. The pins and needles in it were uncomfortable as she grasped it. Her calloused fingers and thumbs brought new life to his once-dead limb. They chattered like magpies as they kneaded more feeling into the muscles of his body.

They left him, and he slept fitfully. He awoke, and it was dark. Laura was in the bed, snuggled close to him. His hand reached out and found her silky bare skin.

"You fell asleep without supper," she whispered.

"I finally knew the truth about healing. Guess I just gave out."

"I know. You are still hard," she said, concerned, as she touched his turgid root. "Such a shame but maybe I can help you without hurting your back—I once had a nasty Comanche do it in my face with his fist," she whispered. "Would it help if I tried to do that?"

"What can it hurt?"

"Don't you strain anything," she said as if gathering courage and scooting lower.

Her hesitant hand gasped his root. The pressure within had become painfully tight. She softly squeezed it in her fist and began to pull on it.

His stiff hips ached to assist her. Forced to submit, he lay on his side and closed his eyes as she began to work it harder. Their breathing increased. He sought her hard breast and rubbed it until the nipple turned hard as rock. By then she was grasping his root in a great pumping action.

"Roll on your back," she said, rising to her knees. Her fury became greater as she bent over her work.

Then he felt her mouth slowly slip over the throbbing head. Her lips begin to pull on the glans. He wanted to drive it deeper, but her hands pinned his hips to the bed as if she knew what his response to her treatment would be. Swirling in the heady pleasure, he strained and felt himself explode like a giant rocket bursting in air.

He lay on his back, and through half-closed eyes studied the dark outline of the branches overhead in the brush arbor roof. His hands combed through her short hair as she kissed his lower stomach and rubbed the insides of his legs.

What was she doing? He felt a new awareness in his flank. Her hands cradling his scrotum and her hot mouth teasing him, he felt a new rising in his shaft.

This time she acted determined to really deplete him. Fighting a desire to pull her on top of his belly, he ran his hand down her spine and soon crossed over her firm butt. His finger sought the wetness between her legs as her hot mouth found him.

The race began. They soared to new heights. A sharp pain increased in his left stone as her hunger for him grew faster and stronger. His finger probed deeper and more vigorously, feeling her muscles contract, and then she pushed harder. He was as deep as his digit could go. A hot flush ran down his hand, and then he strained for another round of cannon fire from the very depths of his manhood.

She crawled up, spent and disorganized, to sprawl half on top of him. No words were necessary. Her firm breasts were driven into his chest. Despite the minimum discomfort to his still-tender ribs, he hugged her close. Drawing a deep breath for strength, he flipped the blanket over them against the cool night air. Things were damn sure going better, he thought as he drew in a sharp breath of the cool night air. *Myra McChristian, we're coming. Don't lose the faith.*

11

Slocum frowned as he set down his crutches. He checked the time by the sun and then glanced at the chief. Bull Elk still hung in his sling in the pool. Usually the man had completed his treatment by then. The chief's eyes were closed, and strangely enough, none of the numerous squaws who rushed about at his least growl were in sight. The Ute had a half dozen wives and beautiful handmaidens that waited on his every wish. Was he asleep?

Slocum was uncertain as he pulled his buckskin shirt off over his head, then unlaced the new leather britches that Laura had finished sewing the day before. Soon he would be riding the yellow horse again. Every time he watched Eagle ride out for the day's hunt, a twinge of envy struck him. The gangly Indian and his friend Bill had become a part of their small family. From the start,

Laura had seen some spark in those two that he had missed.

Disregarding the slumped Indian in the harness, he undressed and then eased himself into the steaming pool. He settled to the bottom, and only his head was above the surface. The pungent sulphur odor purged his nose.

He turned as the Indian mumbled something. Was there something wrong with Bull Elk? He rose to look for someone to help, Heals-Good or one of his women. Not seeing anyone to assist, he waded closer.

"What's wrong—"

His words were cut off by the rage of the man. Bull Elk's powerful hands flew to Slocum's throat and the roar of the Indian's voice reminded him of the angry bear. Though the Ute might be crippled from the waist down, there was nothing lacking in his muscular arms or thumbs pressing with all his might to stop Slocum's air.

His breath cut off, he needed to break the man's grip on his neck. He splashed two hands full of the odorous bathwater in the man's eyes, blinding him long enough to hit him with his right fist hard enough to cave in an ordinary man's cheekbone. The pain shot to his wrist as the man's grasp slipped. Bull Elk began to roar like an angry wounded lion. Still he managed to capture Slocum's upper arm in his grasp, but a second punch to the face spun him loose and twisting in the harness.

"I will have you killed!" Bull Elk shouted. "You have taken my medicine from her. You are well and I am still a cripple!"

Slocum staggered back, feeling his crushed throat and trying to swallow. Laura stood at the edge of the pool with a pistol in her hand.

"What did he do to you?" she demanded. "I heard his shouts and came running."

"Nothing—" Slocum gasped, still holding his throat, not certain his windpipe wasn't ruined.

"What happened?" Heals-Good demanded in Ute, arriving on the scene.

Slocum pointed to the chief and showed her his throat.

She spoke to Bull Elk in their language. Her words were harsh and sounded like orders. Soon some of Bull Elk's women came on the run and hurriedly waded into the pool to take him down.

"I will kill you too!" he screamed as they carried him away.

Slocum carefully watched them leave as he finished drying himself and dressing. He jammed the Colt into his waistband. Then he found a smile as Laura slipped in and hugged him gratefully. Still, the matter of the bitter Bull Elk was not over yet. They needed to make plans to leave before warfare broke out.

Eagle arrived and looked at them. Heals-Good spoke to him, and he nodded that he understood what she was saying. Her visual anger at the breach of peace was written on her copper face as she talked to him in Ute.

"This place is sacred," Eagle finally said. "No one is to make war here. One of his women called her away so he could strangle you himself. He wanted to use your medicine."

Slocum indicated he had heard as he looked toward the camp beyond the junipers. Would the Ute chief try something else?

"She said your medicine would not help him," Eagle said as the wide-eyed Willow and the third woman joined them. They talked among themselves nonstop about the incident.

"I'll get your sticks," Laura said, and started to bend over for them.

"No need for those crutches any longer," he said. The truth of his condition was known.

A loaded report of the pistol from the direction of his camp made them look that way. Soon a fear-faced woman came around the junipers and waved for them to come help.

Slocum heard the others wailing, and he caught Laura by the arm. "There's no need to hurry, Bull Elk has ended his own suffering and frustration."

Laura frowned in disbelief at him as they stopped and let the medicine women go ahead. The three rushed in a wild twist of fringe and braids.

"That wailing is from his mourning wives. I have heard it before in other tribes' camps. The man could no longer accept his fate and has committed suicide."

"That's terrible."

He hugged her to his chest to comfort her.

"Would you have taken that way out?" she asked, crowded close in his arms and looking up at him.

"You must cross rivers when you come to them. If you dread them before you get there, they become wider and swifter. Thank God, I didn't have to cross that one—yet." He arched his still-tender back and put his free hand on his hip. He gazed at the blue sky to offer his appreciation to his maker for the recovery.

"I thanked him too. What should we do next?" she asked.

"We'll get these women some extra meat to smoke and cure. Then we'll head for Colorado and find Myra. We've been here too long."

"What if those two want to go along?" she asked quietly.

"Whatever." He wanted to turn back right then and not go to the dead chief's camp, but they continued toward the tepee across the bare, flat sheets of rock that floored the canyon.

A young woman ran by them, her hands bleeding as she cried out. They watched her throw herself on the ground, wailing and pounding it. She slung blood on her face, hair, and dress as she pounded the ground with her fists.

"What is she doing?" Laura asked, taken aback by the display of sorrow.

"Probably cut off a finger to show her loss for her man."

"Oh, no."

"You never saw that in the Comanche camp?" he asked.

"No, but I forgot many things that they did. It was like I never belonged there." She looked down at her moccasin toes below the hem of her elkskin dress. "I knew someday I would escape or they would sell me back to white people."

"You never gave up? Considered suicide when you were with them?"

"Once I considered it, but I said no, I could endure whatever they did to me. Someday I would be free of them and back with my own people." She hugged his waist tighter.

Some of his wives bore the covered form of the chief from the lodge. Slocum saw an short older woman grasp a long spear beside the door at the sight of him. They stopped, then Laura, realizing the woman's intent, stepped in front of him.

The distance was too close, the woman's aim too good, the time too short for him to push her aside. The lance struck Laura and knocked her backward despite his attempt to move her aside. Weighted down by the lance stuck deep in her chest, she sat on the ground, dumbstruck, and clutched the shaft.

"I never meant this to happen," he said, and jerked the shaft out. The crimson truth on the long keen blade told him enough. The wound was deep and fatal.

"I will miss you, Slocum," she managed to say, and then fainted as the blood spilled over her butternut dress.

"Don't die on me, girl," he mumbled, holding her as he looked around at the blank faces of the women in a circle around him. Even Heals-Good did not offer to help.

She knew his woman had slipped into the afterworld.

Small birds whistled in the juniper branches. Wind swept up the canyon and threw fragments of sand at his face as his eyes narrowed and the moisture fractured his vision. Not Laura. God, don't take her from me. Not the girl who had survived the worst conditions of life as a slave among the Kahwadies, even public rape, and still remained caring and kind.

They took her from him in silence. He rose, strongly considered shooting all the Ute women left staring at him, but instead he walked away down the canyon. More than anything, he needed to be alone. All his time spent healing, instead of the victory that he planned with her, suddenly left him feeling empty, hollow to the very core.

The frost would soon turn the aspens yellow on the slopes above him. He needed to find the Updikes and get Myra back. Somehow nothing ever went as he planned anymore. What should he do next? If he waited much longer, he might get trapped for the winter up there.

Cold tears traced down his face, and he did nothing to control or to wipe them. They were for Laura. He would miss her easy, undemanding company, help, and encouragement in his greatest time of need. Never would he have lived or recovered had it not been for her. And in a flash, she'd been taken from him and this cruel world. *Damn things that happened in life were never just.*

12

"Bill has taken care of that Ute woman who killed your woman," Lone Eagle said as they sat around the campfire.

Slocum nodded that he'd heard the man, but revenge on her killer would not bring her back. They had buried Laura that afternoon beyond the hot springs camp. Her slender, ripe body, wrapped in the colorful Navajo blanket, was placed tenderly deep in the ground with many large rocks piled on top to prevent wolves from digging her up. The three men had worked out much of their loss and grief, digging the deep hole and then carrying huge boulders to cover her grave site.

The site was on a high place, from where one could see for miles and view the endless alpine meadow and pine forest that fringed it. After her nine months with the Comanches on the treeless caprock plain, the solitude and beauty should soothe her. Besides, she had told him often that she liked it in the mountains, wanted them to stay and ranch there, so her place of resting had been fitting.

"Do you wish us to go with you?" Lone Eagle finally ventured the question. Then he poked the fire with a stick, stirring a great arc of red ashes, but he waited for an answer.

"I'm riding north to find the other girl. It may be dangerous."

Bill, his great bulk bent forward to hear his words, shrugged his thick shoulder at the warning as if it were nothing to him. Obviously he feared little in life.

"These Updikes are killers and mean men." He looked at them hard, to impress them that this was no simple hunt for meat, or like Bill killing an old squaw with a pine knot by clubbing her until her pink brains ran out on the dry dirt for stealing the life of a woman precious to him.

"We are not afraid," Eagle said. "We have lived with such before. When you are an outcast, you are safe in no camp."

"You are safe in mine," Slocum said. "I will check with Heals-Good and learn her needs before we ride north."

Both men nodded, satisfied, and looked comfortable with the notion. He felt certain their concern over his acceptance of them was past, and they could get on with their new lives, accompanying him. Strange, how some men wanted such simple things that others would run away from or hold in disdain. He never offered them any money, something most white men would demand, nor did he make them any great pledge. Simply they were free to ride along.

The next morning, when he sought her, Heals-Good asked nothing of them. She looked sad as she placed a hand on his shoulder and spoke in Ute.

"You must ride easy, you are not fully healed," Eagle translated.

He nodded that he heard her words. Then he took the large cartwheel dollar he'd kept in his saddlebag that someone had drilled a hole in and had strung on a leather thong. The coin twirled and shone in the early morning sun.

"This is for you."

She lowered her head to accept it. He placed it around her neck and then she straightened with a nod of approval.

"She says, may your medicine stay strong," Eagle said.

"I am in her debt. I hope she has no trouble with the Utes because of what happened here."

When Eagle explained, she dismissed it. Impulsively, Slocum reached out, gripped her arms, and kissed her forehead. The other two women giggled, so he kissed them too and drew a roar of laughter from his two mounted companions.

"Time to go," he said with a grin.

Eagle rode the roan, his horse carried their pack of bedrolls and dried meat. Bill came behind on his fatter pony. Slocum knew somewhere ahead he must arm them. He could certainly use the new yellow Boys he'd traded to the Kahwadie for the women, if he had them. The first hundred rounds fired from the new model repeaters were great, but they showed wear quickly in the soft metal of their receivers. From experience he knew a worn one was as worthless as teats on a boar hog.

They headed down the great valley between the towering granite peaks that shined in the sunlight. He twisted in the saddle and looked back, but the side canyon was already obscured from his view. To the northwest lay the passage, according to Lone Eagle. With a sigh Slocum settled in the saddle as they trotted their fresh horses.

Midmorning they rested their mounts beside a stream. Slocum considered the silver trout that darted in the clear water. It had been a long time since he feasted on a mountain fish.

"Let's catch some fish and have a feast," he said. They needed a break. And Colorado and the Updikes were still several days' ride to the north.

Bill agreed with a grin and started up the bank. He bellied down on the edge, and his copper arm hung off the bank as he probed the water. Then, as if by magic, his hand came out of the stream with a silver fish of over two pounds flopping in his grasp. A rainbow of color shone in the droplets of water the trout flung in its effort to escape.

"Start fire," Lone Eagle said, and hurried off for fire-wood.

Slocum removed the great knife from his boot and accepted the surging fish as Bill went back for another. Three such fish would be enough for a good meal. Slocum rapped the trout on the head with the hilt and silenced its struggle, then he studied their back trail carefully. Why did he feel they were being followed?

At the stream edge he gutted the fish with his blade, dumping the entrails in the water and then used his thumbnail to clean out the congealed blood down the backbone. Busy with the process, he washed it off in the clear, cold stream as Bill shouted over his next success. He held high a flipping fish of the same size.

Slocum paused and studied the valley south of them. Someone definitely was out there on their back trail. His sixth sense told him so. He laid the dressed one on the grass and then walked back to the bank and took the next fish to clean it.

"Good fishing," he said, admiring the struggling catch.

"Damn small ones," Bill grunted, and his hand went back into the water for another.

"There are kings in this world who would kill for such fishing," he said.

Bill shook his head as he lay in wait. "Never known a king."

"Chances are good you won't either." Slocum chuckled as he squatted in his high-top moccasins and gutted the fish.

"Ho!" Bill shouted, and Slocum turned to blink in disbelief at the huge trout in the man's grasp. It was more than twice the size of the first two.

Bill ambled over with it for Slocum to clean as he finished gutting the second one. Lone Eagle dumped an armload of dry wood on the ground.

"Get another fish," Eagle told Bill.

"Someone else coming for supper?" Slocum asked, not looking up as he slit open the larger trout.

"Yes."

"Who is he?" he asked.

"Not a him, one of Bull Elk's women is coming."

"You see her?" Slocum looked up to gaze down the wide valley. Nothing. He flung the fish guts in the stream and cleaned the pink body in the water.

"She is coming."

"To kill us?" he asked.

"No, she probably wants to go along with us." Lone Eagle held out his hand for a match to light a fire to the dry grass and sticks he had prepared.

"What in hell's she coming for?" Slocum dried his hands and then fetched a lucifer out of his shirt pocket.

"You have a rifle to bring down game. She knows you eat good. A widow is at the mercy of the camp for handouts. She has lived in a chief's camp. Had a good life. Who wants to be a beggar?" Down on all fours, Eagle tenderly struck the match on a rock and then torched his tinder. He straightened on his knees as the flames ignited the tender dry grass that quickly began to lick his pine boughs and sticks into a fire. "You have matches too, so she would not have to rub sticks for fire."

"Ho! Have her fish," Bill shouted, and rose to his knees. Then the burly man stood with effort and brought the trout down to him.

Slocum looked hard to the south and wondered when she would arrive. Pungent wood smoke curled up his nose and stung his eyes as he considered the tasty meal ahead. They might as well wait for her.

13

"She is across the river," Eagle said, not looking in her direction. Slocum agreed with a slight nod as they sat on the ground and ate the delicate trout flesh. She was the tall one, he had seen her earlier, waiting on the chief. Nearly six feet, he recalled her erect shoulders and the full breasts under the fringed deerskin dress, her shapely backside and willowy figure. Pride showed in her carriage. Her own personal respect for herself must have brought her to them.

"So you've got her coming all figured out?" he asked Eagle with a head toss toward her.

"We have rifles and she knows we eat well. She has been a chief's wife. As a widow, she becomes a beggar until someone marries her. Indians like young women for wives, and not someone bigger than they are either." Eagle grinned as if her size amused him.

"She might beat a man up instead of them beating her?" Slocum chuckled at the notion.

Bill nodded quickly, looking amused at the idea. "Her plenty gawdamn tall," he said as he filled his mouth with more trout.

Slocum could see that she rode a fancy piebald horse. He pawed the edge of the stream, impatient as she sat him. A big black-and-white stallion, no doubt her part of the late Bull Elk's estate, or what she had decided was her portion anyway. He also could see from the corner of his eye that she wore a long coat made from prime silver-tip wolf pelts.

"She wants to know if she can come to our camp," Eagle said without looking away from their fire and his meal.

"Tell her to come," he said, then licked his fingers. Stopping to eat these trout had been a good idea, but he still felt a little anxious about this Indian woman.

Eagle waved for her to come over. The black-and-white horse splashed through the stream, and she quickly dismounted and hobbled him. Then, like some sort of royal personage, she drew her shoulders back and advanced toward them.

"Tell her to sit by me," Slocum said, busy feeding himself.

Eagle told her in his indifferent manner. She quickly took her place, her shapely brown knees exposed as she sat stiffly beside him.

"Ask her name."

The man's guttural conversation with her was all but lost on him. He did get the word *cloud* from it. That would be her name. Indians changed their names often in life. This day in the glimmering noon sun they would rename her.

"Tell her that her name is Cloud," he finally said to settle their translating.

Eagle agreed and pointed at her. "Cloud."

Slocum turned to look at her and how she had accepted her new name. She nodded without a smile that she had heard him. Her roman nose had been broken once in her life, but her oval, chiseled face was handsome. A deep burnt-copper color, her lips were a narrow, straight line. Her thick braids were wrapped in elkskin and decorated with blue beads and small blue bird feathers. She returned his stare like an equal. He wasn't too sure, as tall as she was, that she couldn't outwrestle him after his long recovery and the soreness that was not completely gone.

"Tell her to eat," he said, and went back to his food.

At Eagle's command, she took one of the pieces of bark they had for plates and a portion of the remaining fish. With her long, delicate fingers she began to feed herself.

He rose to wash his hands and she scrambled to her feet. He shook his head and told her to sit and eat, pointing at her food. She nodded, but undoubtedly expected to honor him as head of the group. He wondered how she would fit in with his mad army.

At the creek he washed his face and hands in the cold water, then dried them with his kerchief. He started after his yellow horse grazing. She came bounding by him and caused him to stop. Her fringed skirt whipping around her brown legs, she soon overtook the animal who spooked a little, taken aback by her pursuit, and she led him up.

He thanked her and then checked the cinch, tightening it as she looked on very carefully. It would be different to be waited on. The other two were mounting up. She ran and collected her horse and swung aboard.

"Ahead a few hours, there is a trading post," Eagle announced as they swung up a long valley, the snow-capped Rockies rising in front of them.

"Are they friendly at this post?" Slocum asked.

"If you have money they are." Eagle smiled.

"Do they have guns?" he asked, eager to arm his companions in case they unexpectedly met trouble. They would need weapons before he confronted the Updikes.

He twisted in the saddle. Princess Cloud rode at the rear.

"Yes," Eagle said.

"Good, we should stop there."

The trading post looked more like a sheep ranch than a store to him. They rode up in midafternoon as he watched the clouds gathering over the peaks. The weather had been open, but any day they could expect that to change.

A short, whiskered man came out on the log-floored porch, looked them over with a critical eye, and spat in the dust.

"By gawd, I thought that was one of Bull Elk's women. How the hell did you get her?" he demanded, looking wide-eyed at her in disbelief.

Slocum dismounted, looked casually back at her, then at the man.

"Maybe you haven't heard Bull Elk is dead," he said, undoing his cinch.

"Sweet Jesus, what did she cost you?"

"My name's Slocum, I need some supplies." He ignored the man's question and stuck his head in the door, then he nodded to the similar-looking man beyond the pile of cheap dry goods. Toothless and sucking on a corncob pipe, he waved Slocum inside.

"Don't you mind Nolan, mister. Why, he's had two good-looking Ute squaws and they both run off. I told him he wants to screw one, I've got two of them. Gawd only knows why he wants another. Why, he can have either of them anytime he gets hard. It's only right, him being my brother. Howdy, I'm Arthur."

"I'll keep that in mind, Arthur," Slocum said, taking down an iron skillet from a knot on a post and then setting a dutch oven beside it on the crowded counter. He recalled Tom McBeth telling why years ago in Alabama all the Cherokee maidens had married Scottish traders. "Them Scotsmen had all the pots and pans, the warriors had none." The very reason Eagle had given him. Well, he finally had pots for her.

"I need to look at a rifle or two," he said to the man.

"I've got two." Arthur pointed his stubby pipe stem at them on the wall. "Can't keep rifles or guns."

"We'll trade you both of them for her!" Nolan said, almost in his face.

"She ain't for sale." He took the Sharps from the other brother and broke open the breech. The rifling was pitted, but not seriously, nor was the barrel bent from being overheated as many of the buffalo guns were after they were used in continuous shooting.

"How much?" he asked, flipping up the rear sight and taking aim out the front door.

"Her!" Nolan shouted in his face.

"She's not for sale," he said, and set the rifle down. "You got cartridges for it?"

"Maybe fifty rounds," Arthur said.

"Give you twenty-five for it."

"That's not enough, I have to have fifty," Arthur said as his exasperated brother lay across the counter in frustration and pounded his fists on the crude boards.

"Twenty-seven fifty," Slocum said, ignoring the other fussing partner. He held the rifle upright with the butt resting on the bar and waited for a counteroffer. They'd probably traded a drunk Ute out of it for a bottle of cheap whiskey.

"Okay, but it isn't enough. You want to look at the Remington?"

"Yes."

"How much do you want for her?" Nolan demanded.

Slocum shook his head to dismiss the man. Then he took the single-shot rifle from the man. The hammer flopped hopelessly. He shook his head and handed it back. "What about pistols?"

"I've got an Army .44 Colt. Good gun."

"What's it worth?" Slocum asked as the man put the rifle back on the wall.

"Ten bucks." He fetched it from a shelf and placed it on the counter.

"Three bucks," Slocum said as he examined the empty handgun. Not bad, the trigger spring worked. It would do.

"Five bucks. You are hard to trade with." Arthur shook his head.

"Four, and that's all I'll give for the damned thing. Get me some dried beans, some flour, baking soda, and salt too."

"That Nolan is making hisself plumb sick on you trading him that woman," the man said, weighing the beans.

"He can come unsick for all I care," Slocum said, turning to look out the front door to see the man talking nonstop to Eagle and Bill. "She ain't for sale. You got any .44 ammo for this?" He held up the pistol he had obviously traded for at his price.

"Sure."

"I need them too. And some coffee."

"I haven't got any."

Slocum blinked in disbelief at the man. No coffee? Damn, he'd hoped there would be some. The rifle and handgun would partially arm his crew. At least they had some other food besides the game they would kill.

"You don't have any coffee?" He looked around.

"I could spare you a pound."

"Good, put it in my order. I've been drinking Injun tea so long, I've forgot what real coffee tasted like." He looked around, grateful for the moment that the other brother was outside arguing with his men. He sure wouldn't get a thing from those two.

"Comes to thirty-seven dollars, Mr. Slocum," Arthur finally announced after much scribbling on a sheet of brown paper.

"You can have all of it," Nolan shouted as he burst inside. "Just give me that squaw and ride on is all I ask."

"There's your money," Slocum said, counting it out on the counter. He turned to the other brother and shook his head. "She still ain't for sale."

He cradled the rifle over one arm, jammed the Colt in his waistband, and took the two pans. Arthur was sacking his food and ammo in a cloth poke. Off the porch, he stopped and handed the rifle to Eagle, seated on his horse. The man balanced it on his knee and bobbed his head in approval. Then he stepped beside Bill's stirrups.

"Can you use a cap and ball pistol?"

The man nodded, and he drew the handgun out and gave it to him. "We'll load it tonight in camp."

"Here," he said, and held the pots out for Cloud. She dismounted, and smiling as if she had won a big poker hand, took them and raced to the packhorse. She busied herself tying them securely on the packsaddle. Arthur brought her the food and ammunition in two cloth sacks. She placed them carefully in the panniers. Slocum, his back to her as he jerked up his latigos, heard her shout something in Ute. Catching his reins from Eagle, he checked the saddle by shaking the horn and then, satisfied, he swung aboard.

"What did she say?" he asked Eagle, glancing back to see her sitting proud on her piebald.

"Thanks for not selling her to the rat-faced one."

"Tell her when we get out of their hearing that she's welcome."

"A hundred dollars gold for her!" Nolan shouted from the porch, then he spat on the ground.

Slocum didn't bother to answer him and set the yellow horse into a lope. The sooner he left the place, the better he would feel about the whole thing. He glanced back and saw his crew coming on his heels. He turned toward the mountains and felt the cool north wind in his face. The new direction of the force, along with the building clouds, meant a weather change; he hoped it wasn't a big one. The Updikes were somewhere ahead.

He looked back, and his regal princess was riding the black piebald stallion with her braids unfurled, leading the ewe-necked packhorse. That damn fool Nolan had already lost two Indian women. Why risk losing another? Obviously he didn't please them or they'd have stayed at a post with all the supplies that they had on hand. He shook his head and rode into the strong wind.

14

"We should make camp," Lone Eagle said. The snow had begun falling an hour before.

Slocum had stopped them for a consensus about continuing. Cloud had quickly gathered their bridle reins and held the horses. Eagle's tall hat was already white, and Slocum beat his own on his leg to dislodge the load.

"We'll make a lean-to facing the fire," he said.

"Two," Lone Eagle said, and removed a hatchet from his saddle. Bill agreed with a nod, armed with a short ax too, and wearing a blanket followed his partner into the snow-burdened pine boughs.

Cloud had hobbled the horses by the time he went to unload the packhorse. He set their bedrolls on the ground in a pile so he could find them, because the snow was coming down quickly now.

Bill emerged with several poles on his shoulder. Slocum took his ax from him and started to trim a tree to lash the pole across and start the lean-to. She swept up the boughs he cut off and stacked them to use as a fire starter. The shelter begun, she dropped on her knees and began to clean the snow back to make a place for the fire in front of it.

He found some dead branches and dragged them in while she made cedar shavings for kindling with her long-bladed knife. Obviously his working like the others made her nervous or upset, for she looked at him often. He knew that she did not believe that a man would do such lowly things as get wood. He finally squatted down beside her, struck a match to her kindling, and drew a grin from her as the flames began to consume the snowflakes.

Bill brought in a mighty armload of the slender poles to roof the first lean-to with. They rushed to take them from him and set them in place. He turned when they had relieved him of his logs and went back to where Eagle was hacking down more.

One shelter completed, Slocum went opposite the fire to build another one, but she pointed to two trees beside them. Then she indicated the mountains and direction of the storm. He agreed less snow would blow inside the second one if set in that direction; also, it was not where one looked directly into the other one. More private that way too, he mused as he twisted off some of the boughs from the trees and fed their fire with them.

The first lean-to completed, Cloud placed her and Slocum's saddle inside. Slocum tossed his bedroll inside to her and then went off to help the other two bring in the rest of the poles.

The second shelter completed and Eagle's and Bill's things stowed inside, the three men searched for dry firewood to drag in as the blinding snow was past twelve inches in depth and showed no signs of quitting. Next, he knew from past experience, the temperature would drop severely and they needed to be ready for the onslaught.

The only thing that eased his mind was that fall storms and early cold snaps were short-lived. They lasted only a week or so and then usually a thaw came through. They'd have to wait it out. Find some willows or cottonwood bark to feed the horses to get them through this spell. He crouched at the fire. She had on his coffeepot, and it was smelling like honey from heaven. How long since he had real coffee?

Horses secure, they'd find feed for them in the morning if the animals couldn't paw through the cover and find some on their own. She boiled some dry beans he had bought, added some of their jerked meat, and let them stew in her new dutch oven.

Slocum sat on his blankets and smoked a small cigar. How long would the storm hold them up? He hoped not long for the Myra's sake. Cloud brought him coffee in a tin can and put the steaming container in his hands. Squatting down before him, she looked at him hard and nodded that she wanted him to try the hot brew.

Under her close scrutiny he sipped the fiery coffee. It was so hot that it scorched his tongue, but he managed to wink at her and nod—it was damn good. Satisfied, she went to the other shelter and gave the other two men coffee too. For a squaw, she made damn good coffee. He blew on the steam and watched the snow grow deeper.

After their meal she banked the fire with thick logs, the radiation warming their shelter. Satisfied all was in place, she came back to stand before him. She slipped out of her great coat and then grasped her dress at the waist as if to take it off for him.

"No, not tonight," he said, shaking his head, and she nodded obediently. He was in no mood for that. He had not shaken his thoughts of Laura. There was plenty of time for that later. Besides, finding the Updikes occupied much of his thinking.

Somewhere off in the distance, one of the cousins of her coat howled above the storm. His throaty cry made her move closer to him. Grateful for the extra warmth under his blankets, he gave an involuntary shudder and hugged her closer. The wavering red light of the fire danced on the small log roof over them, and he finally closed his eyes and slept. Grateful for her body heat, he awoke once in the night when she slipped out and re-stoked it. Then she returned and snuggled her back and butt against him, and he dropped off again.

Dawn came with more snow falling. Cloud busied herself outside rebuilding the fire and rattling her pans and the coffeepot. Slocum pulled on his boots and wondered how much longer the storm would last.

Eagle was awake. He sat with a blanket on his shoulders and absently watched her work. Slocum slipped over and took a seat beside him, wrapped in a blanket too.

"We can't go far in this snow. What can we do now?"

"Make snowshoes?"

"We may need to do that. How far is Updike's store from here?"

"Maybe two days' walk."

"George Washington once beat the British by attacking them in a snowstorm," he said, recalling the lesson. Could they catch the Updikes napping in such weather? It might be a chance they wanted to take.

"Great father, big chief, huh?" Eagle asked.

"Yes, and he had some good ideas for a small army. Snowshoes, huh?" The white stuff still fell in dollar-sized doses as he considered a surprise attack. Off guard, they might be able to sweep in and take Myra away from them without a shot fired. So much the better, for the Updikes would be fighters in their hole. They hadn't survived this long living in the midst of the Apaches and Utes without being dirt tough.

Cloud came with the coffeepot and Eagle told her in Ute that they were going to make snowshoes. She agreed as she filled their cups. Bill woke up. Huddled in his blankets, he crawled up to join them. Eagle told him.

"Need willow to make the frames," he finally said.

"We rode by some," Slocum said, trying to recall where.

"Not far," Eagle said.

She spoke quickly to him, pointing to the north. Eagle shook his head and explained something to her. It seemed to settle and disappoint her.

"What's wrong?" Slocum asked, enjoying the warmth the coffee gave him.

"She said that their trading post is nearby. I told her that we must go there and get your other woman away from them Updikes."

Slocum looked at the roof of the lean-to. She must think he still had more wives. Too damn complicated to explain in another language, if snowshoes were the answer, fine, they needed them.

This cold made his back ache, or perhaps the riding had done it. No matter, he wanted this whole thing over. He should never have agreed in the first place to come trade the Comanches for a man's daughter.

"Where did she go?" he asked, leaning forward to look in his empty lean-to for her.

"To get some willow," Eagle said.

15

The snow continued, though the flakes became smaller, and the temperature had dropped too. Manufacturing the shoes required longer than Slocum had planned. The willow Cloud gathered was split and steamed, then crosslaced with deer rawhide strips, a process that seemed like it took forever to Slocum.

The first pair was finally finished. Cloud hurriedly strapped them on him. He rose, ready to march a hundred miles, but soon he learned that snowshoes were harder to walk in than he expected. Nonetheless they kept one on top of the deepening snow, and that was their purpose. He traipsed around camp on them, convinced that if the Updikes were close enough, they could launch a surprise attack, carry off Myra and finish this business once and for all.

"How far is this place of theirs?" he asked Eagle as he laced another shoe.

Eagle spoke to Cloud in Ute. Busy steaming more willow over the open dutch oven and its boiling water so it could be shaped, she nodded very seriously, then spoke a few words.

"A few hours on these, she says. She knows the way better than I do."

"I was going to leave her in camp. This may get dangerous. I mean, we may have ourselves a regular war up there."

Eagle translated his words to her. She blinked at him as if she could not believe what he expected her to do. Straightening to her full height, she stopped steaming the willow. With a serious gaze at him, she pointed at herself with the bare barkless strip and then to the north.

He swallowed hard, then agreed with nod. Who wanted to argue with such an Amazon anyway? Besides, it would be dark before they finished making them.

In late afternoon they completed the last ones. Then they had a meal of dried meat and baking powder biscuits made in her dutch oven as a treat. After the meal, they lay down to sleep for a few hours. Slocum planned to use the cover of night to try and sneak up on them.

The cold had deepened when he awoke, but the snow had slackened to a fine spray. He could see outlines of the mountains around them in the starlight. She arose at his first stirring and put the leftover coffee on the fire. The other two awoke. Squatted in the fire's heat, he made certain that Eagle had the cartridges for his Sharps and Bill enough ammo for the Colt. They weren't overarmed. Everyone but Cloud had a gun, and he didn't expect her to fight. One dead woman in his life was enough to last him.

A vision of the angry squaw hurling the spear made him sick to his stomach. The cold biscuit wadded in his mouth. No one must get hurt on this raid. Still, he realized as he washed the bread down with the strong coffee, a danger existed that his people simply accepted.

"Tell her to stay back and be careful," he said to Eagle as they strapped on their snowshoes.

"It will do no good."

"Why won't she listen to you?" He gave the man a wry look in disgust.

"She intends to prove that you need her."

"How the hell do you know that?" He rose and stomped in his broad footgear. They were bound on tight enough for the moment. What would he do about her? He drew in a sharp breath of cold air. Nothing, but go on.

"I can tell by the way she acts," Eagle said.

Slocum nodded that he heard him. He reached down and shook Cloud by the shoulder as she put on her own snowshoes. She looked up. He pointed for her to get behind him. Cloud nodded that she understood him and rose to her full height. She lifted a small pack that she had made from some of the leftover hides.

Eagle got out his bearskin coat for the first time. He looked at Slocum for his approval. Amused at the man's concern, Slocum smiled at the notion and nodded for him to wear it. Bill had on an old, worn buffalo coat. Slocum used a blanket and held the Spencer in his other hand. They started out.

The cold knifed his face and made his nose sore, as he followed the bent figure in the dark, furry bearskin. The snow's brilliance lightened the night sky to day as they fought their footwear. After a mile, they paused and rested close to some dark trees.

Cloud put a hand on his shoulder and pointed to the left side of the valley. His breath recovered, Slocum nodded. That must be the location of the Updikes' place. He drew the blanket closer for warmth and traded hands to hold the rifle. He needed a heavy coat, but he never intended to winter this high up if he could help it.

They pushed on, forced to remove their shoes to cross

a gurgling branch on a dead fall. Then with numbing fingers they retied their snow gear on. The delay made him concerned about what time they would reach the hideout. How strong was their stockade? They might end up locked out after all this marching. And how had the McChristian girl fared?

By this time, Jim Ed had probably given him up for dead or thought he'd skipped out with the two hundred dollars. They mushed along on their shoes, pausing once to repair one of Eagle's. Cloud quickly swung down her pack and stripped out the needed leather. Her long fingers worked nimbly, the shoe was soon repaired, and they went on.

The smell of wood smoke drew a smile to Slocum's face. He could see the cluster of buildings that comprised their fort. Grateful it was predawn, and the Updikes did not seem to have an alert sentry, the assault may not take too long. They sure weren't prepared for a lengthy siege of the place. He reminded himself of that as he switched hands on the rifle.

Cloud moved beside him and took hold of the long gun. They had a small tug-of-war. She indicated she wanted to carry it. He let her have it and then he felt for his Colt in the holster. He undid the thong that held down the hammer and then grasped the blanket on his shoulders shut with both hands. It must be close to zero, he decided.

Great clouds of vapor boiled out of his mouth. His tender ribs hurt worse and the cold air knifed his lungs as he tried to focus on the long low building and corrals. Not much of a fort; good, perhaps they could breach it. Actually it looked more like most ranch stores scattered across the West, but a closer look might prove different.

She stopped him, took the blanket from him, and quickly cut a hole for his head in it. The cold had found his leather shirt by the time she handed it back. He grinned to thank her and quickly removed his hat and then shrugged it on. Why hadn't he thought of that earlier?

Too much on his mind: concern for their safety, the girl's condition inside one of the buildings, and how to get her out with a minimum of fighting and loss of life. His new poncho worked much better to hold in the body heat, but he was still cold.

"Dogs?" he asked Eagle as they drew closer.

"Sleeping."

He acknowledged the answer. Cold as it was, they were probably sleeping with their masters to keep them warm. His heart pounding in his throat, they reached the low porch without being detected. Where did the Updikes sleep, and at which end was the store? They quickly removed their shoes and leaned them against the building. The porch protected by the structure had only a skiff of snow on it, especially close to the wall.

He closed his eyes and tilted his head in a snooze sign for her. She pointed to the other end. Good, they were down on that end.

He handed her the rifle and drew out his Colt. Time for close-range work. His shoulder against the logs, he listened. Nothing. The crunch was loud enough under his soles on the split logs laid down for the porch that he feared to wake the dead as he led the way.

A door rattled and he paused. Someone was coming outside a few feet ahead. Slocum raised his hands to stop the procession. The door flung open to the inside and the party came outside, fumbling around in his fly for his root. A short man dressed in his underwear stepped out to empty his bladder off the porch.

The butt of Slocum's gun dropped him like poled steer, and he crumbled on the ground.

"Tie and gag him," he whispered to Eagle.

Cloud was already on her knees with the pack slung off her shoulder, getting out leather. Satisfied the man was handled, his gun ready, he stepped inside the dark room. It stunk of tobacco, dirty feet, men's sweat, and horse. Obviously the bunkhouse, he stepped over to the first cot, barely able to make out the snoring form, and shoved the gun muzzle in the man's whiskered cheek, ready to smother his protest with his other hand.

Wide-eyed, the man sat up and carefully followed Slocum's silent hand direction to follow him. Eagle quickly bound him and Cloud put a gag on his mouth. He was shoved to the floor and Slocum went back for the next.

He brought more three captives to be bound and gagged. Then he lighted the lamp on the table. Finished, he hissed for Bill to come inside. The big man closed the door, having stood guard outside while they secured the men.

"How many are left?" Eagle asked under his breath as they rounded up the firearms.

"Three brothers, I figure somewhere close."

A dog scratched and whined, impatient at the door. He was no small dog by the sound of his nails on the wood. In a flash Cloud lifted the latch, and when the large Airedale bolted inside, she slammed him in the head with the butt of the Spencer. The dog went down in a pile.

He nodded his approval. Next they needed to locate and take the Updikes. Things were going too smoothly so far. He drew in a deep breath and started for the door. Bill nodded that he was coming.

"You guard them," he said to Eagle and Cloud, then opened the door cautiously lest there be another Airedale outside, waiting. Nothing but the whistling wind as he waited for Bill to step out. They started down the porch.

No latch string on the door. If it was barred, it would require a log ram to open it. If it was held only by a small one-by-two latch, a good stomp with his boot could break it in. Still, there were more doors down the porch that they be could be sleeping behind.

He pressed his ear to the door and listened. He shook his head and then Bill tried to hear by laying his ear to the rough wood. He finally agreed no one was there and they went on to the next door.

A big dog began to growl, and Slocum's heart sank.

"Get up!" someone shouted inside. "There's someone out there!"

"Who?" someone else grumbled.

"Those gawdamn Comanches might be back!"

"What for?" one of the Updikes said. "They've got that gawdamn girl!"

Slocum's heart sunk. Had the Comanches taken her back? He closed his eyes and slumped against the building. Then he straightened, and gun ready, he knew what he must do next.

"Stay put!" he shouted. "We've got your men bound up. There ain't a reason in hell for anyone to die if that girl's not here."

"Who the hell's out there?"

"Slocum and twenty men."

"Twenty men?" someone inside said, sounding impressed.

"Yes, and your big dog out here is disabled. So tie up that other one and save us killing him."

"Go to hell, you no good son of a bitch!"

"You want to die in that room, fine. I can burn you out," he said. "We don't want a damn thing but that McChristian girl."

"I'll kill you, Slocum, you no good sumbitch!"'

"Shut up, Ernie. If he has twenty men out there and our men are caught, we need to negotiate."

"I'd rather die fighting first."

"Then, stupid, go out there and die in a hail of bullets."

Slocum listened closely. There were no more words. Finally the only thing he could hear was the dog's barks and growling at the inside of the door

"What do we do next?" the mature voice asked from inside.

"Tie up that dog to save him. Then open the door and come out hands up. One trick and you all die."

"How do we know he ain't bluffing?"

"Mister, we're coming. Tie that dog up to the bed," the man inside ordered. "And do it good."

"I will. I will."

"We're coming out?" he asked as if the way might not be clear.

"No tricks," Slocum warned, putting Bill on the opposite side with his gun ready. How long ago had the Comanches kidnapped her? While he was at the hot springs, mending, no doubt. The trail would be cold, especially with all the snow on the ground.

The white-bearded older Updike came first, then the grumbling Ernie, and his younger brother followed him. In their pants and underwear tops, they looked around in disgust in the predawn light.

"When did they take her?" Slocum asked.

"Who?" the old man asked.

"The McChristian girl?"

"Over a month ago, Green Horn's lieutenants swept in here and took her like that. She was not a hundred yards from the porch. Nothing any of us could do."

"I told you he never had no gawdamn army out here—" Ernie's tough words were cut off by the sharp jab in the back from Bill's revolver.

"What now?" the elder asked.

"Bill, gather up their weapons, and watch out for that dog in there. I want to be sure they aren't lying about the girl being gone."

"It's colder than hell out here," Ernie complained, shaking as he held his hands high.

"Tell me, I've been out in it all night," Slocum said, and waved them inside, bowing his head to enter behind them.

Cloud came on a long run, and when she ducked her head and entered, the youngest gave a whistle through his teeth. "That's Bull Elk's wife."

"He's dead," Slocum said.

"Yeah, and we heard a bear finished you off two months ago."

"That was a bad rumor. You can believe me, Bull Elk has gone to the land beyond where Indians go."

"How did you get her, then?" the youngest one asked, then began chuckling as if he knew something secret.

"One reason I have her is that I promised her that she could roast your balls," Slocum said, eager to shut the snickering boy up.

She started for him, obviously thinking he wanted him tied up. The boy ran backward, wide-eyed, but in fleet seconds she had him by the shoulder with his arm pinned behind his back. She quickly thrust him up with her leather strips.

"Paw, don't let her do it to me!"

"Shut up or I'll let her," Slocum said as she finished binding his wrists together.

The elder Updike shook his head in disapproval at the boy. The matter was taken care of when she gagged him with a kerchief.

"You owe me plenty, Slocum," the elder one began, boastful. "You blowed up my whiskey and powder at Cordova. There will be a day to get even."

"There will be lots of days, Updike. You think that Green Horn's bunch got her."

"I damn sure do. I'd know that damn lieutenant of his anywhere."

Eagle came into the room with a small squaw in tow. "She says the Kahwadies got that girl."

The tall Indian sat her down on a chair. She cowered and held her head down at the sight of the Updikes. Slocum saw the fear in her eyes.

That made it certain for him that Myra McChristian was back in the hands of the Kahwadie. Damn. He closed his eyes only to open them in time to see Bill's swift boot send the snarling Airedale into whimpering submission under the bed. Slocum closed his eyes to the futility of all his work as his partners finished tying up the Updikes.

Jim Ed, I haven't given up—not yet.

16

At midday, their bellies full of the Updikes' food, they took their leave, Ernie and company still tied up. Five sets of snowshoe prints left the ranch store. Slocum had them burn the rest of their snowshoes so they couldn't immediately follow them.

He had helped himself to a used Hudson Bay blanket coat from the store's stock. There were mittens for all his people, including the short squaw who begged to come along. Eagle agreed it was good idea to take her as the three of them savored the Updikes' private whiskey stock. Slocum added a couple bottles to her pack and took some extra ammo. The little squaw meanwhile cut a large loin from the fresh-killed elk hanging in the kill room.

Slocum helped himself to a double handful of mixed beads from their stock that they no doubt traded a couple of beaver or ermine for. He awarded them to Cloud. She smiled and put them away, then she looked at herself in small looking glass.

"Take it," he said, and waved her on as Eagle tried on an unblocked felt hat.

"Trade with them, yours for it," Slocum said, amused.

Eagle agreed, and left his tilted opera hat on the shelf. Bill found a stocking cap and pulled it down over his ears, the long white red-banded tail bouncing with his braids on his back as he headed out the door.

A few beads, trinkets, two hats, some supplies to replenish part that they'd used getting there—a small price to pay for not taking their lives, Slocum decided, besides all the expense and pain they'd cost him. His tender muscles and the ache in his hips reminded him that he would never have come this way at all, except for them taking the McChristian girl.

He looked back in the late afternoon sun blazing red on the snowy valley and the small shapes of the buildings and corrals. He hoped he never saw the Updikes or their place again.

Where should he go next to look for her? Fort Union and see what the army knew about a white captive? Maybe they had rescued her by this time. In a few days the first snow should melt and they could journey south. Ready for some warmer weather, he carried the Spencer in his hand and trudged along on his snowshoes atop the deep drifts and waves of white stuff.

When they stopped, Cloud took out more leather from her pack and quickly made a sling for the long gun for Slocum. She handed it back and he smiled at her in approval as he put it on his shoulder. Cloud would do to ride the river with.

They finally reached camp long after dark. The two women quickly fried some elk steaks and made fry bread as the men sat around in silence, exhausted by their efforts. Snowshoes standing up at the lean-to posts, he hoped he never needed them again. His legs and hips cried from the strain.

The meal finished, he dug out a fresh cigar taken from Updike's stock and removed a blazing twig from the fire to light it. He drew in the smoke and inhaled deeply. Cloud dropped beside him with a blanket over her shoulders and sat in silence. The other three had piled under their blankets in the other lean-to. Sore and stiff from the hiking over and back, he wasn't ready to sleep.

"Good day," he said idly.

"Good day" she repeated.

He turned and grinned at her. She did not know a good day from a bad one. Tickled at her attempt to mock his words, he chuckled.

"Get the whiskey," he said when he finished his mirth.

She understood whiskey and went to the pack. Quick as a flash, she returned with a full bottle. He removed the cork and took a drink from the neck. The warming effects of the liquor turned his half-frozen ears and nose hot. It burned a trail down his gullet to his belly button, but it was what he needed.

She took the bottle from him and drank deeply, then, looking hard into his eyes, she wiped her mouth on the back of her hand. Not taking her stare from him, he started to take another swig. She said to him in sign language with her long fingers: "Do you want me?"

He squinted, considering the whiskey close by his mouth and how sore his legs and hips were—then he nodded. She rose to her feet in the orange firelight and lifted up the hem of her leather dress. Uncovering her long brown legs that gleamed in the firelight, she regathered the leather in her hands as the curtain rose above the dark triangle of pubic hair. Her flat belly came next, and he yearned to knead the tight cords of muscles that gathered in her deep navel.

At the sight of her full, proud breasts, he finally chanced gulping down a swallow of whiskey. He choked

on it as she lifted the dress over her head. Forcing down
the rest was painful. He recorked the bottle and gave her
a head toss toward the lean-to. He had seen enough; for
certain he wanted her, sore or not.

His clothes proved a formidable obstacle. Not able to
do more than kneel under the lean-to, he fought off his
shirt. The cold air quickly sought him, and finally, when
he was undressed, he dove under the covers and snuggled
to her for warmth. They became like a fiery furnace in
each other's arms, and the concern of chill fled like the
last snowflake on a strong wind.

Her mouth at first like all Indian women's was flat and
unmoved. He knew that they never kissed their men.
Truth was, bucks never kissed their women. But she began to respond to it and soon, as he cupped her full, hard
breast in his hand, she began to use her lips to seek his.

Her strong hands kneaded the muscles of his back, and
some of the tightness fled. His palm slid over her coarse
pubic triangle, and she parted her legs. The wetness he
discovered told him enough. He slipped between her long
legs and then she drew her long stems up around him.

His near-hard root in his fist, he parted the gates of her
womanhood. Probing in her slowly, he fought the increas-
ing desire to forget everything and take her. Her eyes
closed tight and her head far back, she seemed to be sa-
voring his every move into her. Then, as if on cue, her
hips began to gyrate and he went deeper and faster. Her
long arms reached out and her fingers clamped on his butt,
pulling him into her. Soon their pelvic bones were grind-
ing against each other. He was fighting for his breath in
a whirlwind of furious actions. Soft moans of pleasure
escaped her mouth as the firelight danced on the lean-to
roof.

Finally spent, they collapsed in a helpless faint. Still
inside her, the cool air began to seep around the blankets
as he supported himself on his elbows and used the moment to recover his breath. Then her eyes half opened and

a smile touched the corners of her lips as if she had discovered there was to be more. She forced her hips up to him and he closed his eyes to the wave of contracting muscles around his probe. The race was on again. He finished in a blinding lightning strike that caused his back to complain, and he clenched his lower jaw in pain as the last vestiges of his efforts exploded inside her.

Weak and spent, he collapsed on his belly beside her. The sharpness of his hurting forced him to wonder if he had redamaged something vital. Then, as he lay there with the beads of icy sweat running down his face, her powerful hands began to knead his lower back. At first her efforts made him cringe and only added to his discomfort, but in a few minutes the spasm began to go away. Through her efforts the hurting finally subsided and he faded away into a deep sleep.

17

Fort Union lay on an open plain in the warm sunshine. Slocum left his partners camped on the Pecos River and rode up there by himself. They needed some staples that he planned to buy, but he was more interested in learning from the army what he could about the McChristian woman.

He dismounted at the sutler's store and hitched his horse. Two scouts, one white and the other a Shawnee, were seated on the log bench. They both blinked at the sight of him.

"What the hell are you doing here?" the bearded man asked, jumping to his feet.

"Looking for a captive. How have you been, Charlie Dunn?"

"Fine, you remember Dog-Do here?"

"Yes, we were with the Seventh together"

He shook hands with both men, then looked around, pleased that they weren't bantering his name out loud. He had scouted with both these men before with the Seventh Cavalry in Kansas. They didn't seem to be drawing any attention, but he could never be certain, a matter of his being wanted never seemed to escape a certain element on the frontier.

"What kind of a captive? We brought in a white girl last week," Dunn offered. "Let's go have look at her. She may be the one."

"Good, where is she?"

"Over at the doc's house."

They crossed the vacant open parade ground. A few fresh recruits were sweeping the porches of the low log buildings that formed the outer perimeter of the fort. Without a stockade wall around it, the low log, sod-roofed buildings loosely encircled the parade area centered by the great staff with a flapping Stars and Stripes atop it.

A row of whitewashed houses made up the officer's quarters; a row to the side and they stopped at the third house and went up the stairs.

A gray-haired middle-aged woman came to the door. Wearing a fresh white apron over her dress, she smiled at them.

"Ma'am, this gentleman is here looking for a captive," Dunn explained. "And he wondered if the new girl was who he was looking for."

"Come this way," she said. "I'm Dr. Jerome's wife, my name is Addy. I do hope you know this poor child."

"Nice to meet you. Slocum is mine," he said, his hat in his hand as she led him past the staircase and down the hall.

"My dear, you have company," she announced, and stood aside for him to see her.

Her hair had been butchered short with a knife. Hardly past her mid-teens, she huddled in the chair with a tiny red baby nursing at her small V-shaped breast. Even as she looked at the floor in typical Comanche-wife fashion, he felt a sadness for her. It was not Myra McChristian.

"Did she say her name?" he asked.

"No, she's said little of anything since they brought her here. Do you recognize her?"

"No, I don't, but she's not the one I'm looking for."

"My, my. I wonder where they took her from. Perhaps if she knew a town where she'd lived nearby I could write and inquire of officials about her."

He agreed.

"Sometimes I wonder if the army should even bring these poor girls in. She must have been married to one of them. She has that half-breed child. What kind of life can she expect?"

"I don't know, ma'am," he said, ready to leave.

"I think all this talk by the military about Christian principle is mostly to put down in their glowing reports that they rescued another white girl from the savages. And not worried what she would do." The woman looked at him for a reply.

"Yes, ma'am, your idea is not novel to lots of us."

"Maybe being a civilian, you could tell that General Tecumseh Sherman that sometime."

"Maybe, if I see him," he said, recalling a picture of the straight-backed officer and his trimmed beard.

"Well, aside from the newspaper reporters, you're the only one even came to look at her. They took her picture and the flash powder scared the poor thing to death. Thought they'd shot at her. Well, maybe someone will see it in a paper and claim her. But I don't know how they'd recognize her with her hair all cut off and dirty as a pig." She motioned for him to go ahead to the front door. "Don't those people ever take a bath?"

"There isn't much water out there."

"I'm having some soldiers draw up some water right now, and I intend to scrub her clean today. I can't understand anyone liking to be that filthy. She doesn't seem to mind being dirty."

"She's been a captive for a long time."

"I suspected that. What made you think that she was with them for a long time, if I might ask?"

"The way she casts her eyes down. They teach their young girls to do that."

"Will she ever get over that?"

"If she does, it will take years."

"If even then, I suspect. Thank you, Mr. Slocum."

"Thanks, Mrs. Jerome," he said, and then he joined Dunn and the Shawnee at the foot of the stairs.

"Not her, huh?" Dun asked as they drifted back to the sutler's store.

"This one was with Green Horn's bunch."

"Oh, the Kahwadies. They keep avoiding us. We know they're out there, but damn, it's a big country, and I think they can sense when we're coming."

"The army plans to campaign this winter?"

"Sure, we're supposed to have a helluva campaign, but they ain't any easier to hem up than they are in summer, just colder out there is all."

Slocum agreed. He needed to send Jim Ed a telegram and tell him something. No need in him wintering in Dodge. Texas would be a damn site warmer and he was no closer than before to finding Myra.

To ride out on the llano with his small band would be pure suicide. He would have to wait and see if the Comanches returned to Cordova in the spring. Perhaps he would winter there and learn all he could from the Comancheros who returned from trading with them. There was nothing else he could do.

He purchased a new .44 Colt and holster for Eagle and a used muzzle-loading Hawkins rifle for Bill. He included some hard candy for them, dried beans, flour and baking powder, and black powder and lead to make bullets. They had plenty of time to spend waiting, but he wanted to pass the cold season in the village. Too many mercenaries came by such a place as Fort Union; Cordova would be a safer place for him to stay.

He sent a telegram to Jim Ed McChristian, Cattleman's Hotel, Abilene, Kansas.

> Not found her yet. Following leads. Be spring before
> I can do any good. Go home.
>
> Slocum

His supplies in two large sacks over his lap, one on each side, he returned to their camp in the evening. The women had stretched canvas up for a shelter and the thin clouds, he decided, ushered in another weather change. Chances were it would be much less severe this far south than the bad one in southern Colorado. He fed hard candy to Cloud and Sarah, as Eagle called his woman, and drew white grins from both of them as they made supper.

"Where go now?" Cloud asked, looking up from the sizzling meat in her skillet.

"Back to Cordova."

"You going to wait for them to return?" Eagle asked, sitting cross-legged and carefully examining his new pistol.

"Can't do much more."

"Go trade with my people?" she asked, looking for his reply.

"We would need some horses or mules," he said aloud, thinking about the chance of making a profit and covering his expenses. Jim Ed's two hundred was already spent, and his small savings were down to less than a hundred. Trading with the Utes could certainly be a way to make some money and cover the added expenses of the winter and perhaps even spring.

Who would finance such an expedition? He had no idea, but he had an ideal team. She and Sarah could handle the Ute women, who did most of the buying. Eagle and Bill could help him keep things in hand. All they needed to do it were secure a dozen pack animals and a few hundred dollars' worth of trade good stock.

"The Kahwadie have gone back out there?" Eagle asked, rolling the six-gun's cylinder on his forearm.

"Yes, even the army can't find them."

"They are deep in a canyon."

"Canyon?" Slocum frowned at him. Crazy notion, some more Indian tales. The country between them and the Indian nation was flat as any he had ever covered. He figured chances of a deep canyon being out there was only legend.

"I have never been there," Eagle continued, "but a woman who lived with them said that they had deep place in the earth in the center of their lands where the sun shines in the winter. It is always warm there and they are always safe there from their enemies."

"Sounds like a story to me," Slocum said, taking the tin can of steaming coffee from her.

"No, there is such a place," Bill said, breaking his usual silence. "I was there once as a boy. The buffalo and wild turkey are thick as the sagebrush. I have seen more horses than I can count grazing in this place."

"What do they call it?"

"Winter home." Bill shrugged his thick shoulders as if the matter of a name was unimportant.

Slocum dismissed it. If such a place did exist, to ride into a winter campground of that many Comanches would be pure suicide. He wanted to recover the girl, but not get killed trying.

"Someone is coming," Eagle said.

Slocum nodded and wondered who the two riders were coming up the canyon. He didn't recognize the pair as he rose to his feet.

"Powder and bullets are over there in my saddlebags," he mentioned to Eagle, and stepped around the campfire to greet the pair.

"Howdy, gents," he said, and his eyes widened at the sight of the pistol the short one held by his leg. The muzzle came up pointed at him.

"Howdy, yourself," the tall one said, and dismounted. "By gawd, Ned, we got him."

"Who?" Slocum asked, displeased by their actions.

"Listen, Jack Turner, we recognized you back at the fort today. Why, they've got a reward for you back in San Antonio." With that he jerked out the Colt from Slocum's holster. Taken off guard, Slocum saw the man on horseback trying to aim his pistol.

"Watch out, Ned!" the rider shouted.

Too late, Cloud came on the run and batted Ned on the head with the skillet. The sound of his skull meeting the pan made it ring like a bell. Satisfied they were outnumbered, the man on the horse whirled his mount around and went to riding hell-bent back for the fort, beating his horse on the butt with the pistol to hurry it.

"What do we do now?" Eagle asked with a scowl on his thin face.

"I'm not certain," he said, amused at Cloud's stance as she drew back the skillet for a second blow at the moaning man on the ground if he offered any threat.

To stay all winter at Cordova might bring more bounty men down on him. No need to endanger his friends there, though he felt comfortable they wouldn't let anyone take him short of a fight. Someone would get hurt or killed, and he wanted none of the responsibility of that happening. No, they needed to go trade with the Ute, even if it was snowy up there. Perhaps by spring the Comanches would be back and he could try to trade for Myra again.

He was willing to bet that when Jim Ed got the telegram, he thought Slocum was denned up with some luscious señoritas and had spent all the money that he sent him from Fort Union. The hell with Jim Ed; he had to survive the winter somehow. Jack Turner? Who the hell was he?

Playfully he swatted Cloud on the rump and then nodded his approval to her as they headed back for camp. He needed to move around. The proof was out cold on the ground. Damn, was there never going to be any peace in his life?

18

Aguliar Gomez, the mayor of Cordova, leased to Slocum on credit a pack string of animals from various villagers. A mixture of brood mares, a few hinnies that Latinos called mules, and some honest-to-gawd mules was soon recorded and hitched at the rack before the man's store. Next the call went out for packsaddles. The cross bucks and panniers began to arrive in profusion, donated by the same villagers.

"See, we appreciate what you did for us," the mayor said as a woman carrying a rig on one shoulder and the blankets for it in her hands came forward to hand it to him.

"*Gracias,*" Slocum said to her. "I will return it in the spring."

"No worry, we would not ever need it if you had not saved our village." She smiled in a flirtatious way. And then she left with a hip-swinging walk that drew a smile of appreciation from him.

"Your trade goods will arrive in a few days. I have a letter from Señor Goldwaites. He is furnishing them."

"I'll need a list of the fur prices, since none of my people can read."

"I can fix that for you. The Utes have good elkskins and wolf pelts."

"I know something about skins. I spent some time trapping," he said to reassure the man, who no doubt was on the line himself for the goods. "Cloud knows them better than I do."

"Such a woman." The short man looked at the ceiling. "I knew a man once in Conquesta who was my height and he married a tall woman like her. It was said when they were nose to nose his toes were in it and when they were toes to toes, his nose was in it."

Aguliar laughed aloud at his joke, then, recovering, he clapped Slocum on the arm. "But for you, señor, you are so tall, there is no such a problem."

Frost had touched the grass the next morning in the valley. The animals were being saddled in a test at his camp. A red mule threatened to drag Sarah off when she caught it. Bill, in a newfound show of speed, jumped over saddles and gear scattered all over the ground and rushed to her aid. His weight anchored the braying, kicking critter from his backward retreat, carrying the small woman along after him.

Bill soon had the protesting animal eared down and then thrown on his side on the ground. Finished, he sat on the animal's belly and sliced the sweat from his face with his finger as he drew his breath.

"Is that one going to work?" Slocum asked, coming over.

"He'll get better," Bill said with a bob of his head. "He'll be tame when we leave."

"Good," Slocum said with a smile. No doubt that mule

would be a better one when the big Indian finished his intensive training program.

Eagle waved him over to examine a mare's foot that he held up.

"She's been foundered," Slocum said, observing the condition of her frog. "We'd better take her back. She won't make it over the mountains. Besides, she's about to foal," he said, running his hand over her bulging flank.

"The mules would follow her," Eagle said.

"Well, we can't pack her. Use her for a bell mare, then; she could probably make the walk without a pack."

"I will shoe her with rawhide," Eagle volunteered.

"Fine." The cast of pack animals was quickly being assembled under packsaddle by his crew. He looked them over as they were tied on the picket line, ready to load. They would do the job of toting the goods he intended to take into the mountains. As soon as the goods arrived. For the time being, there had been no more signs of the bounty hunters who thought he was Jack somebody.

The tall one, Ned, probably had a headache from Cloud's smacking him over the head with her skillet. Still, the word would be out around Fort Union and elsewhere; there were a lot of damn-sight tougher mercenaries than those two. He'd be glad to be under way, far up the Rio Grande and out of harm's way for all their sakes.

The wagons finally arrived and Slocum felt elated. Dressed in his long blanket coat, he walked about, directing what went where. The teamsters carried supplies to the two women, who packed it all in the panniers.

There were looking glasses, beads, knives, bolts of red cloth, a favorite, Aguliar assured him, of the people. Several small sacks of corn and dried brown beans were packed away. By evening Slocum felt certain they had enough and maybe more than they could take. In Aguliar's office, Slocum and the merchant made books on the items until after dark. His list finally in his pocket, he shook hands with his partner.

"If anything happens to me, Eagle and Bill will return with your animals and stock. They are very honest men and will make you good traders with the Utes in the future, when I am gone."

"I was hoping you would stay." The shorter man frowned in disapproval.

"If I could, I probably would, but that's impossible. Men will come and ask for me. Tell them nothing."

"So it will be." The man nodded, as if thinking hard about the matter.

They left the store, and he and Aguliar stepped out in the street.

"More strangers in town tonight," the man said as Slocum lighted his small cigar.

He stopped puffing on the butt. The yellow light from the cantina shined on the familiar leopard-spotted rump of the Appaloosa horse at the hitch rack. The damn Abbott brothers from Fort Scott, Kansas, were there. Damn, how had they found him so fast? He'd stayed too long in one place.

"Something is wrong?" Aguliar asked.

"Yes, my people will take the goods in the morning. I won't be here," he said, striking alive another lucifer to reignite his cigar.

"Where shall I tell them you have gone?"

"Santa Fe?"

"Sí, amigo."

"You can say I rode to Santa Fe tonight even," Slocum said. He drew deep on his cigar and let the smoke fill his lungs. Then deliberately he slowly exhaled. Yes, he had ridden on.

At camp, she followed him, checking on how he cinched the saddle on the buckskin. She retied his bedroll after him and then stood before him. Finally, when she could stand it no more, she hugged him tight as a bear. Finally she stepped back and he held his finger up—four days and he would rejoin them somewhere on the trail in the north.

She nodded obediently. He swung up and then spoke to Eagle. "These men are bossy white men who shout a lot, but take nothing from them."

"Should we kill them?"

"There's no use in that. They will give up and go elsewhere to look for me. They always have through the years."

A cold wind in his face, he left Cordova, riding north through the desert. On the rise he looked back down at the campfire reflecting from their lodges. It would be warm and snug in her blankets down there. He turned the big horse into the wind and rode into the night.

The third day he viewed the pack train from his high perch. Headed north, he could make out Bill's red-and-white stocking cap as he brought up the rear, cradling the long Hawkins in his arms. He scanned the light snow-covered sagebrush country behind them. If someone were tracking them, they might be as much as a day behind, hoping to surprise him. He waited huddled under the juniper wrapped in his blankets for warmth. If anyone tracked them, he would know in another day, for they were far beyond the normal trails people used for travel.

All he could think about were Cloud's smooth muscular legs wrapped around him and how warm it would be to be under the blankets with her. The day passed slowly, a second at a time. What would he do if the two Abbott brothers came after them?

They would leave him few alternatives: kill them or move on and let Eagle trade with the Utes. That would hardly be fair to Aguliar, since he had promised to handle this winter's trading. His only hope was that the man had been convincing enough that they believed that he had gone south to Santa Fe. The Abbotts were by habit not likely to spend much time sleeping on the ground and trailing him. They chose the comforts of civilization more often than the trail's discomforts. Besides it all paid the same.

A dead man's rich father paid their expenses to pursue him. Instead of giving up after a decade, he still maintained the Abbotts in their hunt. The faded Kansas posters they spread around only inconvenienced him more. At times he'd even considered killing them and telling God that they'd died, but that would only bring on others who might be sharper and more adept at capturing him than the pair. He huddled down in his blankets and shivered. It would be a long wait.

Day worked into night and the chill grew deeper. No sign of the Abbotts or anyone on their back trail. He doubted they would venture up this way in the dark, so he decided to wait until morning and see if they were following his train.

Wolves howled close by, and he spent the night seeking warmth in his wool blankets. Dozing at times, he awoke at others and listened to the night wind and the wolves. Perhaps soon he could join her.

Dawn flooded the land, a small band of mule deer crossed the valley. Grazing and testing the air as they went, nothing disturbed them as they moved in a westerly direction. Soon his horse would require water and attention. He used the old brass telescope to scan back toward the Rio Grande. Satisfied that no one was coming, he rose and stretched close to the juniper. The blankets fell away and he knew the chill would seek his coat.

He rolled up the bedding, satisfied nothing was about. He started for his horse, hobbled in the canyon beyond. Not seeing the yellow horse, he wondered how he had gotten far in the rope hobbles. He stood on a huge boulder and searched. Where had the horse wandered?

There was no sign of him. Was he hiding behind some of the junipers? He looked all around, then went down in the depression where he'd left the buckskin the evening before. Cold and all, it wasn't like the big horse to wander.

He knelt down in between the sagebrush and saw the hoof tracks in the small skiff of snow. Another horse had been there too, and that rider had led his horse away. Who was the rustler? He had little choice but to follow on foot and get his horse back.

How much of a head start did the rustler have? His rifle was in the boot. His food and everything was in the saddlebags, including extra ammunition. He had the two Colts and ten shots, a knife and a derringer in his boot, but they were scant weapons for what might be a long journey. No matter, he needed his horse back.

19

He planned to ration the jerky in his pocket. His own pack train and the others were miles ahead across the range. His own progress was impeded, keeping to cover. The only tracks so far were of the rider, but he dared not venture into the open country, so he moved north along the timber line and scoped the country for the horse thief. If the plan was to kill him, then why had the man not tried that instead of stealing his horse? No, this was to be a match of cat and mouse. The Kahwadie were in those secure winter quarters that Bill spoke about, so whoever his adversary was, he had plenty of time to play the game to suit himself. Lightning Strikes was the first one that came to his mind. A formidable enemy, he would have to be careful to ever survive such a game played by the Comanche's rules.

He looked toward the snowy peaks of the Rockies to

the north. Where was he headed? Perhaps Lightning Strikes did not realize that the pack train he'd been scouting was actually his own. There was nothing to indicate it—with Laura Beth dead, the buck had no way of knowing that he had joined forces with Eagle and Bill since the trade for the two women in Cordova. So perhaps the train was in no danger from him; he must intend for their combat to be man to man. Slocum moved along the edge of the timber, hoping for a sight of him in the vast open country that spread northward.

By noon, with still no sight of the Comanche, he doubted that Lightning Strikes was still in the land. Bellied down on the ground, he used his brass telescope. He searched the far line of timber. Then he viewed a line of white-barked trees in brilliant yellow fall foliage across the basin. Where was his adversary? He revisited the grove with his glass and stopped when something moved. A horse's tail perhaps, then he discovered in his scope the buckskin and a dark chestnut horse in the grove of aspen.

Good, he had found the mounts. He searched for a sign of the Comanche. Where was he? He had to be careful; this man had swooped down on the Updikes and took the McChristian girl out from under their noses. Though he didn't give the Updikes much credit for being the sharpest around, nonetheless Lightning Strikes had taken what he wanted and left them mumbling to themselves.

Did he want a fight? Guns, knifes, spears—there were times that a direct challenge forced the best and worse out of Indians. A Cheyenne challenged in the field of war would single out an adversary and make it one-on-one for the honor, disregarding anyone else until one of them was dead. Slocum knew less about the Comanche than any of the Plains tribes. Still, a challenge to Lightning Strikes's manhood could be all he needed to do to strike up competition.

He hated putting off things that could be settled. On his feet, the cold air turning his breath to clouds of fog, he folded down the scope and then put it in his coat pocket. Next he drew his Colt and fired three shots into the air. Holding the pistol in front of his chest, the sharp smell of spent powder burned his nose. His eyes carefully watched for any sign of his enemy on the far dark line of timber that curtained the steep mountain's face.

Then he saw him. Mounted on his dark chestnut, he held up his shiny Yellow Boy that glinted in the sunlight. Only one rider in sight, he rode back and forth as if challenging Slocum to come on. He fired three shots in reply.

Good. Slocum shoved the revolver into his pocket. Pulling down the brim of his hat, he started down the grade. It made no difference, this matter between them needed to be settled regardless of who was dead at the end. The survivor could get on with his life.

His back ached as he picked his way through the pungent purple sage. A good bath in the stinging springs would ease it, but that was miles away and not likely to be available to him. He could see the dancing chestnut still coming downhill opposite him. Lightning Strikes was holding him back, so their confrontation would be on the flat.

Slocum paused to vent his full bladder. He turned his back to the distant Comanche and looked off to the south as he relieved the pressure and drowned the dry black soil between the brown bunch grass. This basin would be an empty place to die, probably never get buried. A man's bones would be scattered by wolves and buzzards. Folks would only wonder whatever happened to him.

Finished, he laced shut his leather pants. Lightning Strikes was still coming on his horse. Good, this whole matter would be over in the next thirty minutes. There was still no sign of any other Indians, and it was too late anyway, for it was too far for him to outrun a horse back to the timber if they showed up.

He could hear the plodding of the horse's hooves as he descended the hillside. His foot-stomping struck the brittle sage occasionally, and despite the buck's efforts to contain him, the horse still fought to be free. From time to time he gagged on the silver-mounted Mexican spade bit in his mouth. Despite the cool air, his shoulders were dark with sweat. This horse was a great buffalo horse, no doubt taken during a sweep in Mexico from some hacienda owner. The Barb blood was obvious in the wide nostrils, dish face, and the little pin ears. His neck arched under the bit's pressure, and he made a powerful picture as he bore the Comanche wearing his great vest of quills and carrying the buffalo-hide shield that was capable of deflecting even bullets.

Red lines streaked his face, Slocum could see as he drew closer. Paint for them had a purpose—they wore black to trade, but red was the traditional color of war.

"What do you want?" Slocum shouted, just out of range of his Winchester.

"I come to kill you!" Lightning Strikes lithely slipped from his mount. He cocked the Winchester as the horse shied aside, dragging the reins carefully to the side. "It is a good day to die."

"You picked it. Where is the McChristian woman?"

"You must have her."

"Where is Green Horn's white wife?" What did he mean, have her?

"You know where she is!" With a smart grin he gave a haughty toss of his thick braids.

"I paid you for her."

"So?"

"I want my four rifles back. The Comanches are bad traders, I will tell everyone."

"I have come to kill you," he shouted, his feet apart, the rifle in his arms.

"I went to get her from them when I got well from a bear attack."

"You won't need her after today."

"Did Green Horn send you?"

Lightning Strikes shook his head.

"How shall we fight? Guns or knives?" Slocum asked. This conversation was going nowhere; he was ready to get on with it.

"Knives!" Lightning nodded his head in agreement.

He watched him put his long gun on the ground, keeping an eye on him lest he tried to do something else. Slocum drew the great knife from behind his back. Not mistaking his actions, he watched the Comanche do the same thing. The blade glinted in the sunlight that came from over Lightning Strikes's shoulder.

Slocum wished he had sharpened it since last using it to butcher a deer. Any advantage in a knife fight was with the owner of the sharpest edge, which did the most and deepest cutting. There was no time to stop as the Comanche came downhill to the small stream that gurgled through the meadow.

Slocum decided to let him cross the stream. The larger flat was on his side anyway. He closed the gap and took his place to keep the sun at his back.

"Did the bear hurt you?" Lightning asked with a grin.

"Some," Slocum said, eager to get on with the competition. It plainly was down to him and the first lieutenant of Green Horn. Somewhere off down the basin a redtailed hawk screamed his warning. He knew the words— before the sun set this day, one or the other of them would be dead. He planned for the Comanche to be the one winging his way to the buffalo grounds, where all good warriors went, but it remained to be seen.

He threw the knife from one hand to the other and then dried his right one on his leg as he watched the brave jump the small stream and wind his way up through the low sage. His hands dry, he shifted the knife back and forth for his enemy in a show of his deftness.

"A good day to die," Lightning said.

"I heard you. It's a good day for a fool to die."

"Where is the other white woman?"

"A Ute woman killed her."

"So you have nothing to show for your rifles?" Lightning rose to his full height, something he probably had done before with shorter adversaries to show his size and put fear in them. All that Slocum noticed was he strongly reeked of campfire smoke and the bear grease he must have rubbed his bare arms and legs with, for he glistened red under the coating.

"I will."

"Ha! How?"

"Because I am going to kill you. You'd better have warned your spirits that you are coming." Slocum remained in his crouch, ready for the combat to begin. He motioned to a brazen black-and-white bird hopping close to them as if investigating the situation. "That big raven's here because I promised him your balls when this is over."

Lightning rubbed the underside of his nose with his left index finger and frowned. His brown eyes did not move from Slocum, as if he could stare a hole in him. He raised the knife and slashed the air.

"No, white eyes, today you will die." He stepped in, thrusting the knife. Before he could draw back, Slocum slashed his wrist with his knife and a trickle of blood showed on his copper skin.

First blood.

20

Lightning charged with a roar, and they locked both of their knives hilt to hilt. The struggle became one of push and shove without giving one the advantage of knocking the other off guard. If it did happen, it would give the one on his feet a chance to thrust the blade at the off-balance one. Slocum knew his adversary was stronger, and sooner or later, as the push on the knives went higher and higher, he would win this competition.

Maybe he could draw the muscular brave breathing in his face off his guard, he thought, and staggered back a half step as if overwhelmed, and then regained his show of strength. A wide smile began to spread on the Comanche's brown face as his lips parted and his white teeth showed in a confident grin.

A growl from deep in his throat came out with a new surge of power, and Slocum feinted to the right. Thinking

133

that he had overpowered Slocum, Lightning went forward too far, lost his balance, and half fell into his adversary. His brown eyes widened in shock as Slocum's blade sunk in his muscled stomach to the handle.

A hot flash of pain shot into Slocum at the same moment as Lightning Strikes drove his blade into Slocum's buttocks. The Comanche sank to his knees, the blade in Slocum's butt twisted until he used his left hand to shove the man's arm away. The hot steel finally was free of his hip, his own warm blood running down his leg as he used both hands to saw his way to the base of the Comanche's rib cage. Satisfied he had completed the deed, he withdrew his blade. Then, the palm of his bloody hand on the man's forehead, he shoved the blank-eyed buck backward. The Comanche sprawled on his back, gurgling death's song.

"It's a damn sorry day for a man to die," Slocum said aloud as he tried to see the damage in his buttocks. He knew one thing for certain, it was a bad wound. He needed to get to the chestnut horse while he still had the strength and ride for help. At the rate that his blood was coming out, he didn't have much time. He looked at the red-stained knife still in his right hand. The drying blood was already marking up the skin on his hand. In disgust, he threw it away and then limped toward the small stream. He had to catch the red horse; he could never reach the yellow horse far up the mountain. His time was short.

The strength in his arms depleted in the fight, he swung into the crude saddle and started to turn the horse around. No time to catch the buckskin, he could get him later if the big horse didn't follow the chestnut.

Dizzy, he slumped over the saddle, the blood still running down his left leg. He wondered where he should go. His own people had no idea where he was; how many miles north were they? No telling, he had a mountain range to climb before he went after them. His fist gripped the saddle horn as the horse picked his way, his cat hops up the steeper parts hurting him in the Mexican saddle.

How long could he hold on? The light was dimmer, had the sun set? No not yet.

21

He must be dreaming. Naked, belly down, he was in a lodge and Cloud was working on his knife wound. How had he gotten here? He could barely recall the fight with Lightning Strikes, and the wound in his butt made him flinch.

"Lost much blood," she said, sounding concerned as she held a compress tight on his sore backside.

"How did you find me?" he managed to ask in a hoarse voice that shocked him.

"Bill hunt for game. Heard many shots, went to see, but found only dead Comanche Lightning Strikes. Come get us. We find you at dark, where you fell off his horse," Eagle said, squatting on his haunches nearby. "No sign of other woman."

"No, she's probably still with Green Horn," he said,

wincing at the sharp pain in his buttocks from her tending his wound.

"What can we do?" Eagle asked.

"If I survive this, we'll go trade our goods with the Utes, then go find her when it thaws in the spring."

"What if he won't give her back?"

"I don't know, Eagle. I simply don't know." He buried his face in the robe under him as Cloud pressed the wound tighter together to stem the bleeding. He might not live to do anything.

His recovery was slower than he wanted. A few days later she removed the horsehair stitches and each one came out with a hard tug. He gave a yelp at one that came out extra hard and she put her hand on his butt to make him stay.

"You wear pants, no one see this," she teased him.

"Means it must look bad."

"Some bad, you wear clothes, no one see."

"I understand." He buried his face in his arms.

"Who did this?" Her finger traced the scars on his back from the whip lashes. He had never seen the marks, but he full well knew they were there and the fact that they shocked many who viewed or touched them. He had lived through that ordeal vowing to repay his tormentors. He had.

"They're all dead men," he said, looking up and studying the brown valley out the open flap of the lodge.

"Good, like the one who did this to you, he needs to be in the other world."

"He is," Slocum said, watching the sunlight dance on the whirling gold-dollar leaves of the aspens. They had paid with their lives.

Healed enough to ride again, he remained niggled about how the Utes would receive them. Thick snowfall the next day broke the warm-weather pattern and put off their plans to ride north. He was not unhappy sitting in the warm lodge, feeding the fire as the wind whined outside and the large flakes swirled about. Stray snow came in the smoke hole and melted on the warm rocks around the fire ring.

"Do you have a white woman for wife?" she asked, sitting beside him and hugging her knees.

"No, I have no wife," he said.

"Is she pretty?"

"Are you deaf?" he asked, perturbed with her insistence.

"No wife," she mumbled, but did not look at him.

"Are you lonesome for your people?"

She shook her head, but still looked downcast. "I cannot go with you."

"You mean later?"

She nodded.

"No, but I will find a brave man for you."

She blinked her long, dark lashes at him in disbelief. He put his hand on her shoulder and squeezed it gently. She rose to her knees and cupped his whiskered face in her palms.

"I would go with you."

"I would like you to do that, but it won't work."

"Why?" Her brown lower lip stuck out in a pout.

"There are many reasons," he said, recalling the sight of the Appaloosa horse of the Abbott brothers in Cordova.

She turned her face and began to kiss him on the lips. Her firm breasts shoved into his chest, she sprawled him on the blanket. Her hand groping for his manhood under the fly of his britches, her fingers quickly unlaced the restriction as he savored the honey of her mouth.

She shoved down his pants in her eagerness. Then she rose and hoisted her skirt up, exposing her shapely, muscular legs. She stepped over him with a mischievous look, then she lowered herself until she straddled him.

Grasping his root, she started it in her wet tunnel.

Slowly she went lower and lower until she engulfed all of it. Then she began to hunch against his turgid form. Her mouth opened and she began to moan out loud in pleasure. Her head thrown back, her long, thick braids bounced on her deerskin dress and her firm breasts quivered under the buckskin material as she became more involved.

Soon her juices began to flow down his pole and spilled on his stomach and between his legs. He smiled for her sake, enjoying every moment of her actions on top of his belly, though the muscles in his butt were quick to complain. But he could stand it for her.

She rose off him in a flash, stripping the dress off over her head so that her firm breasts shook when she spilled on her back beside him. Out of breath, she pulled him on top of her and soon they were engrossed in a wild union of their bodies. Their breath raging, hearts pounding in exertion, he knew that the end was near and drove as deep as her pubic bone would allow and then the rocket of his attack spewed forth.

Her loud "Ah!" would have awakened the dead, then she relaxed under him. He would have to find her a good man, not just a man, but a real one. Cloud deserved such a mate. She snuggled to him after he arranged the covers over them.

Where was Green Horn and Jim Ed's daughter, Myra? The fact he had let her get taken away knifed him even as the sensuous Cloud crowded her ripe body to him.

The next morning they packed up and headed out in the six inches of snow. Sunlight gleamed off the white blanket and caused him to squint as he stepped aboard the buckskin. Eagle rode the dead Comanche's horse and Bill brought up the rear of the train.

Eagle scouted ahead and he returned in midafternoon with news of a camp ahead.

"Should you go ahead and explain we are in peace and want to trade?" Slocum asked her.

"I will go," she said, and motioned for Eagle to join her. "You stay here. It will be all right, but sometimes braves get excited and take things in their own hands."

Satisfied with her explanation, he nodded to Bill, who was also dismounted, and they watched the pair of them ride off to the north, snow churned up by their horses' hooves. Sarah went about checking cinches and tie-downs on the pack train.

"Plenty good one," Bill grunted.

"You mean Eagle?" Slocum asked absently, watching them disappear around the point of timber.

"No." He shook his head. "Cloud."

"Oh, Cloud, yes, she is a good one."

"You ever sell her, I would buy her."

"Sell her?" Slocum frowned.

"Bill buy her, then." He nodded as though he wanted Slocum to know he meant it.

"You would make her a good man," Slocum agreed, considering the notion for the first time. All he had to do was convince her that Barcelona Bill was going to be a fit mate. How would he do that? Telling her outright might be as good a way as any. He stepped over and undid his cinch and let the big horse blow. His bottom still hurt, and the four-hour ride had not made it any better.

Eagle's woman, Sarah, asked Bill in her guttural tongue if they wanted a fire. Slocum agreed to a small one, and she knelt and cleared a place. Both he and Bill went looking for dead wood. With an eye from time to time in the direction the two had ridden, they dragged up some fuel for her. She had shaved down some cedar wood and had the small tinder ready for the match when Slocum gave her one.

Soon they were warming their hands over the blaze and enjoying the warmth of the sun on their backs. Slocum wondered how long they would be, when he heard horses and shots as well as screaming.

"To the trees," he ordered as he jerked his Spencer

out of the scabbard. Sarah took the lead ropes and Bill went to slapping mules on the butt to hurry them. They might hold out in the shelter of the pines, but they had to hurry, for it sounded from the screams like an entire army was coming. He drew up the cinch and swung aboard the buckskin. Damn, he had worried about this, his gaze centered on what would soon round the corner of pines about a half mile west of them. He wouldn't have long to wait.

22

She came into view first. When he saw the large group of bucks riding around her, he didn't dare shoot. A quick glance and he saw Sarah and Bill had the horses in the trees. Good. Then he saw her wave to him, and he frowned. More rifle shots and one buck had an old pistol he must have saved to blast the sky with. What was happening?

"They come to welcome you," she said, out of breath, riding up, and slipped from her horse.

"Damn," he said with an exhale. "I figured they'd come to eat us."

"This is Blue Horse Man," she said, indicating the one under the full headdress. "He is Slocum," she said for the chief's benefit. Both men acknowledged each other with a nod.

"Tell him I will bring the train back. We thought they

were mad at us when we heard them coming, shouting and shooting.''

Her translation brought a roar of laughter from the bucks on horseback. He crossed the snow in long strides; it sounded like they were going to be all right. Utes were odd, he had dealt with some in times past, and one never knew if they were going to be peaceful or not, depending on the last dealings they had with some other white men. Obvious Cloud knew something about her own people. Perhaps they could trade most of their items and go back to Cordova. It would be damn sight warmer down there than up in these mountains.

Blue Horse Man held a council in his tepee, and everyone puffed on some of the worst tobacco Slocum could recall. The lodge was thick in smoke. Each man in the circle took a deep suck and then blew out the smoke from the ornate foot-and-half-long pipe. Big medicine, but damn, wherever their tobacco came from, it was sure rotten by his standards.

Did he know the Comanches? The question was posed and he nodded, letting Eagle tell how he had killed Lightning Strikes. Many rose up to better hear the words of his translator and they looked impressed that he and this lieutenant of Green Horn's had such a match and he had lived to come there to trade with them.

After several speeches about the various men in the tribe's bravo, Blue Horse Man called for food and a strong drink made from fermented corn furnished by the women, who served everyone. Cloud was among the servers, and brought Slocum his plate. She also gave him a cup that contained the sour-smelling pulpy concoction the Utes drank. More a brew than liquor, nonetheless it was like their smoke, not very palatable to his tongue.

The trading began the next day and the squaws had many fine pelts saved from the season before. They were well cured and he felt certain that his suppliers would be happy with their quality. Cloud led the trading and he observed her firmness with many of the barterers.

The supplies dwindled by the day's end, and he knew they would return to Cordova with a surprising amount of robes, skins, and pelts. Slocum saw the man under a blanket coming; big and burly, he filled out the blue wool blanket he used for a shawl, something ringing familiar about him.

"His brother, Big Boy," she hissed, rushing to him.

"Bull Elk's brother?" he asked, seeing the family resemblance.

"Yes, and he mad. Not make Big Boy chief."

"Nice," Slocum said, undoing the thong on his Colt and then using his arm to sweep her away from before him.

"He kill you," she insisted.

"No," Slocum said, stepping forward to meet the man as he swept the blanket aside, exposing his breechcloth and vest. Defiance on his face, he stood a few feet from the blankets spread on the snow to trade on. Too damn cold to do such a thing unless one expected to be involved in great exertion.

To his right, Slocum heard the Spencer click and he shook his head for Bill's benefit. He must handle this disposed heir to the high seat of the tribe himself.

"You speak English?" Slocum asked, advancing forward.

"Me want her," he said, and pointed at Cloud. "My brother's wife is mine."

"She does not want to go with you."

"Then I will beat her until she does," he said, taking a whip from his belt.

"No." Slocum held up his hand. "She is already married to a man."

"You?" The man pointed his whip at him.

"No, Barcelona Bill is her husband."

"I kill him, then."

"No, kill me, then him. Did you come to die here?" Slocum asked.

"I come to get her. My brother's wives are mine."

"She chooses to be with him."

"I am not sure who she is with. It makes no mind, she is mine." With that he tried to pass Slocum to reach for Cloud.

The barrel of his Colt jammed into the man's hard gut, Slocum met the hard glare. Big Boy's bad breath was close enough to almost smother him as he gave the revolver a last hard shove.

"You want to die?"

The man reconsidered, and then he stepped back, but none of the anger or hatred fled his face. In fact, he looked blacker than before as he considered his next move. It was fight or retreat. The latter seldom satisfied the Indian mind, and Slocum knew that chances were good that if the man were to save face before all the hushed crowd, he might have to charge him to keep his head up.

"I will have the council settle this," he said, and stomped off.

For a long time no one spoke or moved. The path through the rank of women looked like the wake of a deep canoe parting the still waters. Slocum knew his men were coming forward, each armed with rifles. Cloud stepped beside him and spoke softly.

"I stay with you and others," she said. "Not him."

"Would you marry Bill?" he asked, seizing the opportunity and satisfied she would be treated well by him. "Yes."

He never looked aside toward her. He waved for the Ute women to come forward and trade, then he nodded to himself—the matter was settled, she would go with Bill.

Cloud came past him, talking loudly and encouraging them to bring their wares to trade with her. He holstered the Colt mechanically and watched her shapely butt under the leather dress as she began bartering with her customers. He sure hoped that Bill was up to that much woman.

He moved to get some more goods from their horses as Sarah unloaded another pack.

"Did you think she meant it?" Bill asked, shoving the Spencer into the scabbard.

"Yes, traders have all the pots," Slocum said, then he winked at the grinning Bill. He drew out a cigar to settle himself.

"Pots?" Bill asked with frown.

"You will be plenty of pots for her," Eagle said, motioning toward her and then grinning at him.

"Good," Bill said.

"She likes to eat every day and not to be beaten with a whip. You remember that," Slocum said, and went after the last pannier with the big Indian on his heels. He drew on the cigar as he went through the slushy snow. They might trade the entire pack train if things held up. He exhaled the rich smoke. This trading could prove to be very profitable for Eagle and Bill. They had the right squaws to trade with the Utes, and Cloud could make tough barters.

"Me carry. Bad for back," Bill said as he hoisted the canvas container from the cross bucks.

"Thanks," Slocum said, and drew again on his cigar. Big Boy would have some last word, but perhaps his solution would work. He wondered, as he slung one arm over the packsaddle for support and drew on the cigar, where Myra was. Somewhere out on the caprock. Maybe in the deep sheltered canyon that Bill spoke about where winter never came to the Comanches. There could be anything out in the vast unsurveyed reaches of upper Texas, including some deep canyon. Nothing would surprise him.

Near sundown, a messenger came from Blue Horse Man. Slocum was needed at the council was how Eagle translated the man's desires. He considered what they might do about his problem and finally decided the course. If Bill wanted her, he could speak to the Utes.

"Bill!" he shouted to the man busy packing furs in a pannier. "Come, we must go speak to them about your woman."

"Do you need me?" she asked him softly.

"No, Barcelona Bill must tell them that you are his woman," he said.

If she understood or not, she nodded and then straightened. Her firm breasts made the deerskin blouse tight as she threw her shoulders back. He felt a sinking in the pit of his stomach. Damn, he had parted with lots less women than Cloud, but to deliberately give her away . . . Then the thoughts of the Appaloosa came to mind, and he nodded at her grimly. It was the only way.

In the council lodge they again smoked the terrible pipe slimy with everyone's spittle, and the dreaded taste was as bad as he expected. The only hope was that their sour beer would wash it away later. He passed the pipe on to Bill, who sat beside him, hoping he had taken in and blown out enough of the foul smoke to please the Utes.

Big Boy started his oration. The whole thing meant little to Slocum; he saw the others listened like jurors did at a trial. Big Boy pointed repeatedly at them, accusing them of much, and drew nods from the assembled on many of his points. Slocum knew how a foreigner must feel on trial in the U.S., understanding little. He hoped the big man beside him knew more of the situation than he.

Big Boy finished with a hellfire and damnation conclusion the likes of which Slocum hadn't seen since he went to a brush arbor camp meeting in his youth, when a fiery Baptist preacher tried to save every soul in Alabama.

"You understand what he said?" he asked Bill.

The man nodded thoughtfully and with some effort rose to his feet. He gave the chief a salute with a partially open hand, then he nodded to the rest, turning in the center of the tent as if to indicate he wanted to recognize them. He went across the room and jerked Big Boy to his feet, shouting something in his face, then threw him back against the great tent sides.

Like a great lumbering bear he came back and sat down. A titter began to spread through the council of warriors sitting cross-legged. They whispered and then they laughed louder.

Slocum watched Big Boy pick himself up and coyotelike slip out the flap. Satisfied, everyone was amused by Bill's action. He leaned toward the man to question him.

"What did you tell him?"

"That she was my wife and he was not getting her."

"That seemed to work," Slocum said, considering this as he began to chuckle.

Blue Horse Man ordered food and drink. He saw the smug grin in the corners of Cloud's mouth when she entered the tepee. She brought them each slab plates of steaming meat and vegetables. In front of him she knelt before Bill, setting Slocum's plate down then, using her long fingers, she held the bark plate up for his inspection.

He nodded his approval and let her feed him a choice morsel of meat with her fingertips. Their stares frozen on each other, the room grew very quiet as elbows gouged the inattentive to pay attention to the display. Satisfied the mood was set, she rose and went for their drinks. Slocum busied himself eating as the whispering went on around the circle of Utes. Few eyes missed her proud walk or shapely calves among the other women moving in the circle to feed their menfolk; Bill busied himself eating.

"Someday I will pay you," Bill said between bites. "For her."

"A gift, my friend."

"No, someday I will pay you."

"What about Big Boy?"

"He has been disgraced three times. They not made him chief, you did it, and now I have done it. He will leave this camp and go elsewhere."

"I wished I shared your confidence."

Bill nodded confidently for his sake and then took the cup from her. "Plenty good."

"More food?" she asked.

"Yes," he said, and handed her the bark. She did not even check with Slocum, but he was full enough. Satisfied that his Indian maiden had a good man, he would be free to go search for Myra. What else could he do to find her? He wondered if Jim Ed had wintered in Abilene despite his telegram and if the hotel he was staying in had heat. It would be good to get back to Cordova and some warmer weather than the Rockies held. A shiver of cold ran up his spine, and on top of that he had lost his bed partner. That thought made him even colder as he drank the sour brew from the cup.

23

"Oh, señor, you are back so soon," Aguliar shouted as he ran alongside his horse. "I see you are very loaded with furs. But so early, are they any good?"

"Last year's." Slocum drew up his horse in the warm sunshine that bathed the town square. "Yes, they are prime pelts and well done."

The little man hurried past Cloud and Sarah to the packhorses and his finger fumbled the ropes. Bill dismounted and moved him aside to undo the hitch and lift up the tarp for the eager man.

Eagle winked at Slocum as if this were their private joke.

"Oh, *sí*. Are they all this good?" the mayor asked, rubbing the fine fur of a fox over his face.

"Maybe better, I'm going after a drink," Slocum said. "You boys help him unload his merchandise." He dismounted, loosened the girth as he looked over the dancing little man with scarfs of fur around his neck as he went from pannier to pannier as if in a trance. Slocum was glad he was so damn happy. A wrap of the reins, he hitched his buckskin and went into the cantina.

"Pour me some of your bad whiskey, amigo," he said to Elandro, and looked absently around the room for any threatening person. Seeing only locals, he let him pour a glass full.

"So you are back without the girl?" Elandro asked in low voice.

He nodded his head and then he downed the glass of brownish liquor. Following the fiery liquor with a deep exhalation, he reached for the bottle and poured himself another.

"The Comanches stole her from the Updikes before we got there."

"The other girl?"

"A crazy Ute squaw killed her the first trip out." He shook his head ruefully. Poor Laura lived to be free of one tribe and killed by another, protecting him. *Damn.*

"Is there someone here who knows where they winter?" he asked flatly.

Elandro's eyes widened and quickly he put his finger to his mouth. "No one must speak of this place. The Comanches would cut out our tongues. How did you know of it?"

"Men speak of it." He considered the next glass of whiskey before him. If there was a guide to get him there, maybe he could find the Kahwadies and take her away from them. He had little to lose. Chances were by spring Green Horn would take his people out on the caprock or across the llano to raid more Texas ranches.

"There is a man named Gallo who has been there," Elandro said in a low, guarded whisper. "He lives in the village of the weavers and once was taken captive and lived as a Comanche for many years. He has been there."

"He lives in Chimayo?"

"Yes, but he might not—" Elandro dropped his gaze
and shook his head that he was not certain. "Do not tell
him that I told you."

"I'm going to see this Gallo in the morning. Now I am
going to eat with Maria and then I'll get some sleep in a
hammock tonight." He raised his eyes to the ceiling as if
to ask if the bed was available.

"*Sí*, you may sleep up there," Elandro said, then went
to answer a drunk's request for more liquor.

Slocum lighted the fresh cigar and walked down the
alley toward Maria's café. Bone weary, the whiskey had
settled him. His boot soles creaked on the gritty caliche
ground.

"Put your hands in the air," a voice challenged him
from the side of the building he had passed only seconds
before.

The Abbott brothers had lain in wait for him. He closed
his eyes. Did his friend the mayor know they were there?
If he did, so did Elandro, his so-called friend in the bar—
no one stayed in Cordova without knowing. He blinked,
for the man holding the pistol was hardly twenty-one.

"Who the hell are you?" Slocum demanded.

"Just get them paws up," the kid ordered with his gun
barrel, reinforcing his directions.

"I said who are you?"

"Mister, for five thousand dollars I'm the king of
France," he said, drawing the small Colt from his holster.

"Those Abbotts promise you that much," he asked,
then began to chuckle. "You've been taken in by them.
That reward ain't any good, it's run out."

"Mister, I been waiting here almost two months for
you. All I got to do is send the word and they'll come
busting up here from Santa Fe and pay me."

"You've wasted a big part of your life, son."

"I don't figure so. I've done a lot of things for a damn
sight less than five thousand dollars."

"Sad thing is, you'll never collect it."

"Your pals ain't getting you out of this, Slocum."

"Can we go eat? I'm starved, and besides you've got my gun."

"One trick and you're dead." The hollow-cheeked youth tried to look tough.

"Hell, you've got my gun. What am I going to do, stick you with my Barlow?"

"You keep moving and keep them hands where I can see them." He motioned Slocum on.

So the Abbotts had promised him big money. Why, they'd pulled that trick before and never paid the one who brought him in. Grim reality, it was good enough for the greedy bastards that worked for them. Capturing him was always too swell a deal for anyone to pass up. One word from this kid, he said, and they'd hotfoot it up there from their cozy rooms in Santa Fe, take the prisoner, and leave the bounty man without a stitch of money. He knew after the short walk to the café that he would never convince the kid that he was about to be taken for a sucker by the Abbotts. Good enough, he owed this skinny kid nothing.

They entered the restaurant and Slocum drew a frown from Maria. The kid, not seeing it, motioned Slocum to the booth and then sat down across from him, placing the revolver on the table at his right hand.

"Hands on the table," he ordered, then turned to the pale-faced girl.

"We both want steaks, potatoes, and fresh tortillas," the kid ordered, his right hand resting on the handgun.

"What to drink?" she asked, glancing concerned at Slocum and then back at the kid.

"Coffee." He looked at Slocum.

"Fine."

"It will be a few moments," the girl said with a small quiver in her voice. She hurried back to the kitchen.

"You weren't planning on going anywhere, were you, Slocum?"

"I guess not." He sat and settled down with his hands folded on the tabletop.

"Keep them right there," the kid said sharply, and almost reached for him. At the last moment he must have reconsidered his action; instead, he settled for aiming the Colt at his heart in threat. "You'll die in here if you try anything with me."

"What name do you go by?"

"The Verdagree Kid. Why?" His clear blue eyes had the coldness of a winter wind.

"Just makes it a lot more friendly to converse with someone you know, kid. I guess you're going to spend that money on a good time, huh?"

"Yeah, I am. I might go up to San Francisco or out to that new big silver strike in Arizona."

"Tombstone, they call it."

"Yeah, I heard about it." He acted a little indignant that Slocum thought he didn't know the name of the place where he was going.

"What will you do if those Abbotts don't pay you?"

"They're dead men."

"That suits me," Slocum said as the girl brought their coffee.

Disappointed, he watched the kid use his left hand to raise the mug up to sip it. Mark one down for the Verdagree Kid; he had hoped for the switch. But there was plenty of time left. They drank their coffee and then the girl brought them large browned steaks, steaming potatoes, and a plate of snow-white tortillas. Wringing her hands, she asked if they needed anything else.

"More coffee," the kid said, and she nodded and went for the pot.

"How did you become an outlaw worth that much?" the kid asked, cutting his steak in pieces with the sharp knife resting atop the plate.

"Good question, and why it is all a big hoax. They want me because they're getting day wages and expenses for trailing me. There simply isn't any reward that big for me.''

''I heard that,'' the kid said, clumsily feeding himself with his left hand, his right one on top of the Colt.

Slocum nodded. There was no way to convince this stupid boy of anything. It called for more serious work. He took the coffee cup freshly refilled and steaming in his left hand. Then he tossed the hot contents in the kid's eyes. In a flash with his right hand he drove the steak knife through the web of the kid's right hand and pinned it to the tabletop.

Calmly he drew the handgun back, set it beside his plate, and went on eating, ignoring the kid's screaming and jerking.

''Sit down boy,'' he said, leveling the gun. ''You're about to upset my supper, and I might have to kill you if you don't do like I say.''

The kid slumped in the seat, grasping the wrist of his pinned hand. Blood began to spill on the tabletop from the wound as he squirmed in his seat. ''Please take it out, mister. Oh, for God's sake, take it out.''

''I repeat, sit still, and when I finish my food I will consider it. You need a good lesson on the people you are messing with. This bounty hunting gets dangerous.''

''Oh!'' he cried, half raised in his seat as he held the pinned-down hand and wailed. ''It's killing me!''

''No, but this gun will if you don't sit still and behave.''

''I hear you,'' he said with a shuddering breath, his hollow face paling as the pangs of hurt drew on the muscles of his jaw.

Slocum savored the steak and the potatoes. Then he ate the kid's biscuits in small bites before he ate his own and finished the meat slowly. Any moment he figured the kid would pass out, but he was fighting it. His left hand was clenched so tight on his other wrist, the knuckles were white.

"Now, when I let you go, you ride fast as you can to Santa Fe and tell the Abbotts that I said they were pig shit!" Slocum wasn't satisfied the boy had heard him. He knocked his felt hat aside, got a handful of his greasy hair, and jerked him up in his face. "Tell them I called them pig shit!"

"I will," the boy said stonily. Slocum reached down and drew the knife and hand up from the table.

"Oh," the boy gushed.

"Pull your hand out. They want their knife back."

The boy fought the knife off as Slocum held the handle, pushing down with his left hand until the blade was free. Then he fell out of the booth on his knees, groaning and grasping his wounded one.

"You got three minutes to get out of Cordova," Slocum said.

"I'm going. I'm going." He rose, staggered to the door, falling once to his knees and then rising with great effort.

"I never knew he was in Cordova looking for you," the woman apologized, coming from the back and wiping her hands on the floury apron.

"No problem, it will be a long while before he tries his hand at bounty hunting again. How much do I owe you?"

"Nothing. You have done this village so much. I am only sorry about what he tried to do here."

"Maria, enough is enough." He left a silver cartwheel on the counter for her and her girls, crowded in the kitchen door, eager not to miss a thing.

He lighted a new cigar in the doorway and then waved to the fine-looking dark-eyed girls in the café, busy cleaning up the blood and mess. In the late afternoon sun he drew deep on the smoke and then repeated the man's name—Gallo. He would go see him at first light. A cool wind reminded him that winter was still at hand, but there was a breath of warmth this far from the mountains.

24

He rode into the village of Chimayo as the rooster crowed. Huddled in his blanket coat, he passed several uncoated adobe houses and took the right fork, crossing the stream that gurgled beneath the hollow-sounding plank bridge. They had told him that this man Gallo lived in a house with a green front door on the left under the leafless ghostly cottonwoods. From several places, yapping cur dogs chose to make a run at his horse, then they circled short and ran back as if their guard duty were complete.

He spotted the green door under the eve of a low-roofed adobe hut. After a look up and down the deserted road, he reined the buckskin in the lane between the plots of green winter wheat that struggled in the shallow furrows.

He dismounted heavily and tied the buckskin up to the arbor. Checking about and seeing no one, he undid the cinch and then took a seat on a board bench to wait for them to awaken.

With some effort he pulled off his left boot and straightened the sock wrinkled under his sole that had bothered him since he left Cordova. Had he been walking, he would have addressed the warp sooner, but riding, it had aggravated him only on the trip over. Seated, he brushed off the bottom of the sock and then used the mule ears on his boots to tug on while he shoved his foot deep in the vamp.

"Señor?" a soft voice from the partial open doorway asked.

"*Sí.* You must be Señora Gallo?" he asked, busily bent over and stomping to get his boot on. The job not completed, he stopped to talk to her with his toes halfway in the right one.

"*Sí,* but what do you wish?"

"I need to talk to your husband when he awakens." He removed his hat to speak to her.

"Are you from the sheriff?" She frowned, holding the blanket close at her throat. She looked younger than he thought this man's wife would be. She had full, cushiony lips that looked ready to kiss at any time. Her eyes were big as brown saucers and her cheeks were long, giving her a beauty from both her Indio and Latino blood. The blanket served to protect her from the cold and no doubt cover her nightdress. It hid her figure as well from him too.

"No." He shook his head to dissuade her of any concern. "I have work for him."

"*Sí,* I will wake him—"

"No, I can wait," he said to dismiss her concern as he bent over and struggled again to pull his footwear the rest of the way on. "I will wait here until he awakens and then we can discuss business."

Finally his heel slid in place, and he tested it, rocking

back and forth. To his chagrin, he discovered that the sock had another wrinkle in it. Damn.

In a short while she came outside dressed in a colorful dress with a wool shawl on her shoulders. She was very wide-hipped and short. The low door was no obstacle as she brought him a steaming mug of coffee. He guessed her barely five feet, but many people in the villages were no taller. She had ample breasts under the shawl, which overall made her look like an inflated hot-air balloon he'd once seen in Kansas at the end of a trail drive, and it caused some cattle to stampede. An angry range boss threatened to shoot the dude down if he went over his herd again. He wondered if she ever floated away on windy days.

"My husband is dressing, señor."

"*Gracias,*" he said, and blew on his coffee.

"Señor?" the man said, coming from the house and putting up his galluses. A nice-looking man, clean shaven, dressed in the simple unbleached clothing of the agrarians. Hatless, his thin black hair ruffled in the cool morning breeze that swept the valley. Perhaps five foot six, he was slenderly built, but no doubt muscle-hard from fieldwork.

"My name's Slocum, Señor Gallo. I come to hire you to take me to the canyon of the Comanches."

The man looked around in panic to see if anyone had heard him. His dark face paled and his eyes widened. He began to shake his head to dismiss the very notion of his suggestion.

"There is no such a place, señor."

"Los Canyon del Comanches," Slocum said as if the sound of the words were enough to intrigue him. "I come to get you to take me there."

"I can't. I forgot the way."

"Ah, I see you have a nice woman here. Children?"

"No." Gallo shook his head. "Someday maybe, they come. We try hard." Then he grinned at Slocum and they both shared a moment of manly amusement.

"If you will get me close—"

"They would kill me for such a thing." Gallo stood with his arms folded, unmoved and unswayed.

"How much to buy a new team?" Slocum asked. He had seen no draft animals and wondered if the man had any. "Perhaps if I pay you twenty American dollars for two young ox."

The man acted deaf. He remained silent, still unmoved by the offer.

"I will pay you that much to show me the trail to get me there." He studied the man for any sign of weakness, wondering what would make him give in and agree to scout for him.

The man looked at his moccasins and slowly shook his head. "I could never do such a thing. They would learn and kill me in my bed."

"I will find you a matched pair of steers."

"But dead who will need them?" His dark eyes narrowed as he stared in disbelief at Slocum.

"When I can find the way there, then you can ride back." He needed to shake the man's hangdog attitude, and since the oxen as a bribe seemed about to work, he wondered if he should press it more.

"They would learn I did it and kill me for leading you there." His eyes narrowed to slits, and he looked at Slocum as if he could not understand his desire to go there.

"No." He tried again to convince the man. "They will think I found my way by mistake."

"No, they can read signs in the dust like a book and they will know someone led you there." He shook his head vehemently.

"Señor," his wife said, coming to the door with a tray. "I have some fresh flour tortillas dipped in cinnamon and sugar."

"*Gracias,*" Slocum said, accepting the plate.

Gallo took one and wolfed it down as if still in concentration over the matter. Slocum wondered how close Gallo was to accepting his offer.

"Can you tell me how to go, then?" he asked.

"I can ride for a ways and then point you. But if you tell them I did that, they will come slit my wife's throat, and mine too, while we sleep."

"They will never learn a thing from me. When can we go?"

"I have no horse or mule."

"I will send one over this afternoon and we can meet above Cordova on the creek in the morning. I will have a packhorse."

"The steers?"

"Yes. I will arrange that the mayor Aguliar has them when you return."

"You must tell no one what we do. I swear, if they even hear of such a thing—"

"No one will know our business."

"I will go pray today that no one knows."

"In the morning I will meet you. My man will deliver you a good horse that you may keep."

"It is a fool's trip. They will kill you." Gallo looked at him warily as if he were offering an out for him.

"I know that, but I must try to find her."

"I understand, then. If my wife were there, I would do anything too."

"Good," Slocum said, not feeling it necessary to explain more about Myra to the man. He might believe him completely crazy and not go at all. Better he suspect that his efforts were higher in nature than a mere job.

He finished his coffee, recinched the yellow horse, and started back. Eagle would deliver the man a suitable horse and he would arrange with Aguliar for the oxen in Cordova. He would need a packhorse and provisions. Would he take more guns to trade or not? He couldn't decide as he set heels to the buckskin's sides and loped eastward.

Dawn the next morning was a dark purple as he sat on

his horse in the cedars, hunched under a blanket against the frost, looking for the rider to come from the west. The packmule snorted wearily and stomped his feet in the cool morning. Loaded and ready, he hoped to make a long swing past Fort Union and get out on the caprock. The military frowned on unlicensed folks trading with the Indians even more so trying to recover a white woman, a job they considered their exclusive jurisdiction. Obviously, like the rest, they had not done much about Myra. Both Eagle and Bill had requested to go with him, but he wanted his strike force small. Better to go unnoticed, since the only way he could get her back was by stealth. There was no way to trust that Green Horn would again trade her back to him and live with his transaction.

He spotted the long-legged Comanche horse coming up the shadowy road with a rider under a sombrero. Gallo was well seated on Lightning Strikes's mount. Fresh and ready, the sorrel came at a running walk. The small man huddled under a brown wool serape in the saddle drew up in front of him.

"Good morning," Slocum said, moving into the road.

"I hope that it is a good one and we have many more," Gallo said, checking around as they sat their horses.

"It will be. I have arranged for the steers to be here when you return," Slocum said.

"I hope I live to work them."

"You will, come on."

Slocum rose in the stirrups and trotted his horse. The black mule came on an easy lead, and they headed up through the hills toward the yellow slit that marked the horizon. *Jim Ed, we're going looking for her.*

25

A towering bank of clouds hung in the northwest. They crossed the grassy caprock, moving in an easterly direction once past Fort Union. They paused to water their animals at a lunar lake, one of the many depressions without an exit that gathered precious liquid for man and beast. The Comancheros came upon the caprock only when assured they could water at such places. They sent scouts out ahead to check on such sources before they committed their cart trains to venture out and trade with the Comanches, a tradition Cordova had kept for centuries, that they were forced to put aside under U.S. law, but they still chanced it, for the trade remained critical to their livelihoods.

The edge of the lake was fringed with thin ice as they refilled their canteens and let their mounts breath.

"Any sign around here?" he asked, leaning on the seat

of his saddle and studying the azure sky and vast horizon before them.

"There was horseman here a few days ago. He did not let his horse drink and rode on."

"You saw that in the dust and grass?" Slocum asked, impressed with the man's ability.

Gallo nodded as if that were nothing.

"You lived with them for long time?"

"From a child until I was a man."

"Why did you leave, then?"

"I did not like my belly to be hungry. I wanted to see my grandchildren and I recalled the Virgin Mary and Jesus. There is no room for the old in a Comanche camp. I once saw a man bash in the head of his own mother with a stone."

The wind was all, besides the stamping of their horses, that Slocum could hear. Gallo had more to say to him. "He said her tits were long dry and she no longer made babies. To feed her was a waste."

"I know that they wanted only the healthy."

"It is why they steal so many women for wives. Many die in childbirth, others the hard life kills."

"So you rode as a warrior."

"Yes." Gallo nodded. "We often went to Chihuahua and stole many women and slaves down there. They made better wives than most white women. The Mexican women were tougher and quicker to accept a new life."

"You had a wife?"

"Yes. When she and my firstborn died at birth, I rode away from the camp and found my way to Chimayo. I could never live like that again."

"You belong to the Catholic Church?"

"Yes, and I have prayed for being so savage. Father says I am forgiven."

"Good," Slocum said, and remounted. The clouds looming behind them were the harbingers of a big snow. They needed to hurry and find the Kahwadie camp. Blizzards could rage out there like they did when he was scouting for Custer and the Seventh up in Kansas. He wanted no part of such storms.

A few hours later, they caught signs of a great horse herd, and Gallo dismounted. He broke open several horse biscuits in his hands and checked the contents of the apples.

"These are Comanche tracks," he said, squatted in the ground.

Slocum joined him, and a twinge of excitement ran up his spine. They were getting close to them.

"Is this near the canyon?"

"No."

"What are they doing out here, then." He frowned, upset at his scout.

Gallo shook his head. "I don't know, but they are horses that have not eaten grain. They are Indian horses."

"How close are they?"

"Maybe one, not more than two days ahead."

"Good," Slocum said, wondering if the man expected to be released after getting him this close. He never mentioned it, and they rode on.

"There!" Gallo pointed to a thin streak of black smoke curling skyward.

"That a camp?" he asked.

"No, they would never leave such a signal."

"It's some damn thing burning, isn't it?"

Gallo nodded, and they both whipped their horses. The cured grass rolled and waved like an ocean as they drove hard.

Slocum could see the blackened wagons and the slaughtered draft stock shot full of arrows like pincushions as he drew up his horse. The wagon bows looked like the rib cage of a coyote after being burned to a crisp in a prairie fire. He dismounted with his revolver in his fist. There was nothing left alive. A facedown man had been scalped, the strip of stone white in the burned remains of his hair. Another blackened body had been viciously mutilated, then tossed on the burning wagon and it hung over the half-burned box.

Slocum fought the sourness rising in his throat. In the center of the ring were piled-up chests and crates, no doubt set up for protection. There, a body of a thin woman sprawled naked on her back, no doubt multiply raped and then tortured. Her pubic hair had been scalped. Beyond her, two other women's bodies had been carved up with vicious knifes until their identity was gone. In a daze of shock, he stumbled out of the enclave, unable to stomach looking any longer at them.

Six wagons in a train, perhaps a dozen men and boys had defended it. They had oxen and horses for draft animals. The Comanches had taken perhaps some children and maybe other women. Then in the burned-out wagon he spotted the small body of an infant burned to a blackened crisp.

He rushed from the circle of wagon to where the fire had stopped, dropped to his knees in the thick grass, and retched until the dry heaves shook his shoulders. Tears blinded him as he watched Gallo on his knees nearby, fervently praying.

The worst past, he jerked the kerchief from around his neck and wiped his lips. Clearing his throat and spitting several times did not remove the burnt-copper stench from his mouth and nose. He wished for a good drink of whiskey, but there was none in his saddlebags.

"Is this why they aren't in their canyon?" he asked the pale-faced Gallo.

"They must enforce their way on the invaders. They ran the Apaches from the plains and the Utes too. They think they can do it to the Americans." Gallo shook his head and then looked him in the eye. "You still ask why I left their camp?"

"No," Slocum said, stepping into his stirrup. "No way

we could bury all of them. A damn shame, but we better get on.''

"There will be more.''

"I know, but that's the damn army's job, not mine. I want one girl back.'' There, he'd said it—he wanted one girl and he would ride away when he got her. He had no war with these bastards. Myra was all he wanted.

Snow began to fall in the next hour. The flakes grew larger and their visibility lessened. The white whorls of howling wind and snow forced them to dismount and use their horses for shelter.

"Leave them saddled,'' Slocum said, unsure how they would survive the blizzard. They had no fire or fuel. His feet and hands were already half numb from the cold.

"We'll wrap up in our blankets is all I can see to do.''

Gallo nodded, starting an avalanche of snow from his thin shoulders as he fought with red fingers the strings holding on his roll.

They'd be damn lucky to live out this bad a storm. The temperature would fall to zero, and the wind would whip up the snow in piles higher than a man on horseback. Someone might find their bones come next spring. No fire concerned him as he rationed out corn in the muzzle sacks for the animals. Maybe in their tiny world they would survive, between Gallo's prayers and his deep thinking about how dumb he was to come out here in this season.

Even a cold hotel room in Abilene was better than this. His hands inside his tent of blankets thrown over his head, he rubbed them on his shirtfront for warmth. *We're out here looking for her, Jim Ed.*

SLOCUM AND THE COMANCHE TORTURE, 172

26

Someone was coming. Slocum threw back the blankets and rose to his feet in a cloud of snow. The two horses were watching them approach.

"The damn army's found us," he said ruefully to Gallo as the man sat up and frowned to ask him who was out there.

"You would think in all this blankety-blank land and blasted snow we could have avoided them," Slocum said, ready to throw his hat down and stomp on it.

"What will we do?"

"Play stupid."

Gallo nodded that he understood the plan.

A lieutenant in a new blue overcoat and fur cap rode up, accompanied by a red-mustached sergeant and two corporals. They looked snug and warm in their winter uniforms as horses and men alike issued clouds of vapor when they breathed.

Slocum hugged his arms and danced on his half-frozen feet for some warmth. The officer looked fresh from West Point, and that would not help their situation. New graduates did everything by the book and being out there without a official permit made it look like he and Gallo were either gun or whiskey runners.

"Gentlemen," the officer said. "My name is Samuels and I must see your papers."

"Papers?" Slocum closed his right eye against the glare off the snow and looked pained at the man, as if he didn't understand the request.

"I didn't catch your name?"

"Slocum."

"Mr. Slocum, there is a federal requirement that you must have a permit from the Indian Bureau to be on this land."

"Me and Señor Gallo here are looking for buffalo. Is that against the law?"

"Yes, unless you have the proper papers."

"What kind of papers? Ain't this part of the United States?"

"This, sir, is reservation land."

"Damn, we never passed no signs, did we, Gallo?" He looked at his partner.

The man shook his head.

"Enough is enough. Sergeant O'Malley, arrest these two men and we will let the federal courts treat them and listen to their story."

"I'll have to ask for your weapons," the big noncom said.

"This is highway robbery," Slocum complained, hoping to catch the attention of the officer, but the shavetail was looking eastward. He reached in, drew out his Colt, and handed it to the man. Gallo shrugged and the sergeant patted him, then straightened, finding no weapon.

"You will be forced to ride with us for the next few days," Samuels said, then waved his column forward. "Our mission is not completed out here."

"I know you from somewhere, Slocum," O'Malley said with a grim set of his mouth that made his mustache roll. His green eyes studying Slocum, he finally nodded at his discovery.

"You scouted for the Seventh in Kansas."

"You scouted for Custer?" Samuels asked with a frown, checking his horse and coming back.

"I was there," Slocum agreed.

"Sir, this man is a very good scout, better than any we have."

"Do you know these hostiles?"

"No, but Gallo here does."

"Could you find a large band of them if I, say, overlooked this trespass charge?"

Slocum looked down at the snow. He had the upper hand; he had to use it right. If those blue legs went charging in that camp, they might get her killed. If he could get her out before they got there—maybe. Damn, it was too cold to think. He hunched his shoulders.

"Lieutenant, get us some warm clothing and we'll find you a big camp of them. Right, Gallo?"

The short man nodded perfunctorily.

"How far away are they? Colonel Yancy has a column coming from Fort Sill to cut them off in the east. We could wedge them between us."

This boy was bucking for captain's bars. He didn't give a damn about Colonel Yancy or anyone else. He'd seen the same greed for glory in Kansas. At West Point they'd taught Samuels how to fight, and he'd missed the big war. This was the last place he had to prove himself. Give him a Comanche camp to strike, and he'd whip the hell out of them or die trying.

Good enough. He had the power and chance. O'Malley

handed him back his weapon, then he gave his own pistol and holster set to Gallo. A corporal went back and got them both wool overcoats, fur hats, and gauntlet issue gloves.

"These items of clothing must be returned at the end of your service to the army," Samuels reminded him as they hurriedly put on the heavy outerwear.

"I don't aim to be buried in it," Slocum said, pulling on the gloves.

"What *do* you plan?" the officer asked, impatient with the delay.

"You make camp here. We'll go ahead, find the hostile camp, and come back as fast as we can and get you. It will have to be full speed ahead when we find them. They can move fast even with large numbers."

'I know that. Which one of the bands do you think is ahead of us?"

"Green Horn."

"Whew." Samuels exhaled out loud. "Slocum, you find him. I'll get you a big medal."

Pleased with the man's words, Slocum knew the fever for a higher rank would bring him and his cavalry on the run. Perhaps in the confusion he could rescue Myra. Desperate, but times were that. Another bad storm might leave the both of them frozen to death.

He mounted his buckskin and hung his felt hat from the horn. He saluted the lieutenant and rode out with Gallo close on his heels.

Out of hearing of the army, Slocum sighed deeply. "Reckon we can find them?"

Gallo fought to get his too large glove back on his left hand and smiled. "Somewhere."

"You warmer?"

"Much better, *gracias*."

"Thank me when this is over. We'd better trot these ponies."

In late afternoon, the bloodred sun stretched across the

white-blanketed earth when Gallo stood in the stirrups and
turned his ears to listen.

"What is it?"

"Stallions screaming."

"We close to their horse herd?" Slocum asked.

Gallo nodded. "They are a few leagues ahead."

"Good, let's get down and eat something. Then we will
split here."

"Why?" Gallo frowned. "We must ride back and tell
the lieutenant."

"You're going back to tell him. That'll give me most
of the night to scout their camp, then you bring him up
here fast. If I don't have her out by then, there won't be
anything left."

Gallo agreed with a firm nod.

They ate some crumbling cheese and chewed on some
tough jerky. The water in their canteen had frozen, so with
his mouth too dry, Slocum wallowed the jerky around and
tried to draw up some saliva. Unsatisfactory was all he
could manage to think about the matter of their supper.
Never mind, he was close enough to try to recover her—
*damn, Jim Ed, I'm freezing my butt off out here, hope
you're warm wherever you are.*

27

Slocum had heard the animal whistle in the far side of the camp. That sounded like the most excited and the most vigorous of the many tethered stallions about the camps. He slipped beside the tepee, and his knife ready, looked around for any sign of a sentry. The Comanches were overconfident, there were none in sight. In a snatch, he caught the lead and sawed the rawhide braided leaser apart as the big horse snorted in distrust at him. The taut rope snapped under his knife blade, and the startled stallion half reared and finding himself loose, tore away for the distant herd.

No time to revel in one success, bent over, he headed for the next one, a fiery piebald paint. Slashed loose, the horse churned snow all over Slocum. His muscled hams stuck his hooves hard into the frozen stuff and he threw more in wads as he raced to find the mare he had smelled in heat.

"Yeah, go get them," he said in a half whisper as he hurried to the next tepee and there released two more stomping males. Already the sounds of the stallions fighting shattered the night.

A guttural "what is going on?" from a lodge forced him to duck down as a big, powerful buck tore out of his lodge in only his breechclout and moccasins and ran out across the snow to see about the horses fighting at the large pony herd.

Other braves joined the man, and they too raced afoot for the tribe's herd as Slocum rounded a tepee and slashed loose another animal. The camp came astir. His time left would be short as he hurried across the crunchy snow to the great lodge of the chief that was twice the size of the others. Four horses were stomping at each corner of the great shelter, and he cut two loose in a flash. The third one showed his teeth and tried to paw him. His first swipe with his knife missed the rope and instead cut loose the other stallion. A wide-eyed roan almost flung himself down on his side in a panic to escape Slocum's wild efforts.

The worked-up roan struggled to his feet in a fury of flying snow. He charged the still-restrained sorrel with the snapping teeth of an alligator. In his charge, he knocked the other stallion to his knees. His mouth wide open, he seized the sorrel by the neck and mane. With the fury of a bulldog, he began to shake the other horse in his mouth like a rag doll.

The red horse tried to buck loose from the painful bulldog hold of the other male. Unsuccessful and still tied, he jumped and dived, but the roan held tight. His pained screams brought the great chief of the Comanche rushing out of his shelter. He hefted a great spear from beside the doorway. Holding the spear end toward himself, he began whacking the roan on the head and ears with the handle.

Dodging the plunging horse, Green Horn almost lost his footing to save being run over by the two fighters.

His voice shattered the night as he shouted for them to quit. Despite turning his head to deflect the blows that the chief managed to apply, the defiant roan kept his deep bite. Time and again, the chief's voice louder, he danced in and out, popping the defiant roan on the head with the butt end.

Worked up into a fury, the roan had raised an erection and planned to punish the other male in his grasp with it. Slocum crowded close to the side of the tepee and watched, hypnotized. The roan intended to use the smaller horse for his own pleasure, and the fat chief of the Comanches was not doing much to him as he struggled for his footing and shouted louder at the stallion to quit.

Then the big man slipped in the snow, his moccasin soles slick from the frozen stuff underfoot. He scrambled to his knees and then up as the sorrel, still in the bite of his opponent, came around and began to whimper in pain. Unable to escape either the rope or the roan's teeth, he was wearing down.

Green Horn, despite his size, scurried like a prairie dog. He rose, roaring from the bottom of his lungs, and began again to thrash the roan with the handle end of his weapon.

The hurting sorrel swung his rump around. Green Horn tried to step back and dropped the lance. He held the point out inches from his belly, looking for another place to rush in and punish the roan. The other end of the lance's handle struck the sorrel's hip, and the force of the pained horse's motion drove the razor-sharp point deep into the big man's gut, impaling him on his own weapon. Holding the embedded shaft in his grasp, he staggered backward, screaming so loud that the earth shook.

"Myra McChristian!" Slocum shouted, and slit the tent open like an eggshell. *Girl, if you're in there, this is no time for hesitation. We've got seconds to escape this place.*

Three women screamed and crowded to the far side.

"Where is the white woman?" he shouted at the top of his lungs. It was dark in the smoky interior, but none of the blank-eyed women looked like Myra. Then they panicked, and dragging their small children, ran screaming from the lodge. He had only seconds to flee. Where was she? Damn the perfect plan. He kicked a pile of furs into the wall and swore to himself and his bad luck. Then he drew his Colt, stepped out of the newly made door in the side, checking for anyone. Nothing in sight, he ran from the tepee. His time was up.

Out of breath, he reached the buckskin, but he could hear the thunder of hooves as the large herd of ponies rushed away across the snow.

"Good," he said to himself, vaulting in the saddle. The ponies had stampeded in the confusion. He reined the yellow horse around. Now all he had to do was find Lieutenant Samuels.

Why wasn't she there? He shut his eyes for a moment at his disappointment. Where had she gone? Was she dead? He owed Jim Ed an explanation. The man would never believe how hard he'd tried and all that he'd been through to try to locate her. He whipped the yellow horse to send him racing across the white stuff to the west. Somewhere that shavetail West Pointer should be coming on a hot foot. That even sounded good, anything warm would be delightful as the bitter cold air made his eyes water. He would never complain about a hot day ever again. He whipped his reins from side to side and then filled with dread, he glanced back over his shoulder to see if anyone was pursuing him.

They were. At a considerable distance behind him, there were riders on his trail. Leaning forward on the horse's neck, he urged the buckskin to go faster. He considered shooting at them, but that would only be a waste of ammunition that he might need later. *Hell, Jim Ed, I hope you know someday that I really tried to rescue her.*

28

The buckskin was about to give out. Moans issued with
his gasping breath told Slocum that he would soon be
through. He kept looking ahead across the broad white
starlit horizon for any sign of the army. The Comanches
were still on his tail. Perhaps he had a half mile between
him and them in the pearly whiteness. He could hear their
yip every once in a while above the buckskin's hoofbeats
on the snow and his hard breathing. His own life was in
Samuels's hands. Where the hell was that shavetail?
Damn, he could have brought slow mules up there by this
time.

Whenever the yellow horse went down from exhaustion
or a misstep, Slocum thought of the Spencer and five shots
in the Colt on his hip and the same in the revolver he
carried in his boot. Any minute he expected to have to
shuck his stirrups when the spent horse's heart burst or

he stumbled. More than anything, he hoped he landed easily enough in the white stuff so he could recover in time to face the bucks hot on his heels.

The horse slowed. It was time to make a stand. He jerked the horse's head to the side in a last-ditch effort to provide himself some cover. He wondered if his savage pull on the bridle would do what he needed to trip the horse and sprawl him on the ground. In a flash he jerked loose the Spencer from the scabbard, only seconds before the buckskin's nose plowed into the crust. The pony's front leg went out from under him, and he fell, spilling Slocum out over his head into an icy bath that blinded him, flakes of frozen snow filling his eyes.

He pawed at his face and kept ahold of the rifle in the cradle of his arms. Damn, he had to see them. They were only a fraction in time behind him. On his knee, he tried to make out their forms against the sky through the sight on the rear of the Spencer. His eyes filled with ice and crystals, they blurred as he fought to see an outline of the first rider. Then he fired and the lead horse screamed and rolled end over end, throwing his rider to the side.

The second warrior came screaming with all his lung power. A soft-nosed lead bullet caught him in the chest and took him off the lathered pony that raced by so close to Slocum that he threw himself to the side to avoid being trampled.

He rolled on his back, ejecting the spent shell and levering in a fresh one as he struggled to half rise to shoot. No time to aim, he pointed the muzzle at the third screaming buck. Perhaps a boy, his lance struck the snow only inches from Slocum as he fired the rifle from his hip. The rider went off the far side and struck the snow hard enough, he knew that he would never get up.

Then he heard more horses as he rose and whirled, the Spencer's butt in his hip, and replaced the spent round. The army had finally made it.

"Any more hostiles here?" O'Malley asked, holding his hard-breathing horse in check.

"No live ones, but you'd better hurry. I stampeded their horse herd, so they should be easier to round up."

"Forward ho!" the noncom shouted, and the troops rushed by Slocum.

He used the rifle for a post to lean on as the army filed past him. He saw Samuels pass, but he had nothing to tell the man and was grateful when the lieutenant rode on with his men.

"That you, Slocum?" Gallo asked, reining up his horse.

"Yeah, help me catch one of these loose Indian ponies. My horse is done in."

"Sure," Gallo said, taking loose a reata from his horn. He soon returned with one of them on the lead.

Slocum struggled to unsaddle the hard-breathing buckskin lying prone on the snow. He knew what he must do for the animal. The job would not be easy; the big horse had saved his life and given his all to get him there.

"He can't get up?" Gallo asked, dismounting.

"You got that forty-four?" Slocum asked, considering the caliber a better eliminator than his .31 caliber.

"Sí. The army gave it to me."

"Give it to me."

"Sure, but—"

He hefted the heavy six-gun in his hand as he looked at the dark eye of the horse sprawled on the snow, his hard breathing a raspy whistle. Unable to swallow the hard knot in his throat, Slocum cocked the hammer and squeezed the trigger. Its report reverberated across the frozen plains. The buckskin went still, then his powerful hind legs gave a few final kicks and his last breath escaped in a grateful rush.

Slocum handed the revolver back. He swept up the saddle and went to toss it on the Indian pony. Even as far as the white-eyed horse had run, there was enough spook in him; he shied. Slocum had to chase him in a half circle to get the rig on. Finally, the girth in place, he mounted the wiry pony and reined him up.

"You ready to go?" he asked Gallo.

"We shouldn't help them?"

"You want to go kill some Comanches?"

Gallo shrugged and rode up close. "I thought—"

"Piss on Samuels. He wants captain's bars and we may have made that possible. I stampeded their horse herd."

"Green Horn won't—"

"He's dead. Got stuck in the belly with his own spear."

"You killed him?" Gallo frowned.

Slocum considered his question for a long while, then he shook his head. "No, the son of a bitch killed himself. Let's ride, I'm so damn cold and hungry, I may never ever warm up again."

Gallo kept looking back as they rode west, until finally he drew up alongside Slocum's stirrups.

"What happened to the woman?"

"I cut open that tent and expected her to be there. Boy, did I have a shock."

"Was she alive?"

"Damned if I know. She wasn't in his tepee is all I know."

"What will you do now?"

"Wire Jim Ed McChristian and tell him I did all I could. He can sue me for his damn two hundred dollars. Come on, I want to find a fire and get warm again." He turned up his collar and set the pony into a trot. Coldest dawn that he could ever remember being up for.

29

He found Eagle, Hawk, Bill, and Cloud camped up the creek from Cordova. Several lodges set up, he dismounted in the warm afternoon sun, noticing the mules all looked well kept and the horses hitched on the picket rope were shod. They had done well and would make good traders. His pride over their success made him swell a little with satisfaction.

"Hey, anyone around here?" he shouted, looking around, and then dropped out of the saddle.

Her face beaming, Cloud stuck her head out of the flap and shouted his name. The others came outside and rushed to shake hands or hug him, depending on the gender.

"You saw the Comanches' winter place and lived?" Eagle asked, taken aback by the fact.

"I'm here, aren't I?"

"Was it like I said?" Bill asked, eager for him to verify it.

Slocum shook his head. "I never made it there. But Green Horn is dead—" He blinked when another woman came out of the lodge and straightened. She carried a small infant wrapped in a blanket.

"Myra McChristian?" he asked, feeling too weak in the knees to stand.

"Yes," she said, looking down.

"Girl, you are a sight for sore eyes."

She only kept her gaze cast downward.

"She escaped Lightning Strikes and wandered many days. Some hunters brought her down from the north and we heard she was with a family on the Red River," Eagle said. "So we brought her here for you."

"You have done a good thing," Slocum said, putting his hand on the tall Indian's shoulder.

"Myra, your father is waiting for you in Abilene."

She shook her head.

"Yes, he is. I promised him a grandchild. He wants that scamp and you both."

She raised her head up and the tears spilled down her face. He stepped over and hugged her and the small baby. *Jim Ed, I've found her and she's coming home.*

Two weeks later in Santa Fe, he had put Myra and Jim Ed the second on the stage for Abilene. Jim Ed couldn't sell his cattle and had wintered in Kansas, so he answered their first wire.

Slocum stood in the shadows of the porch as the coach prepared to depart. From the window she smiled at him and nodded as he touched his hat.

"Read all about it," the paper boy shouted, coming down the boardwalk, hawking newspapers. "Chief Green Horn is dead. Comanche war is over!"

No, it wasn't over. One band of Kahwadies was captured. He was busy dismissing it when the eastbound stage bolted away. Across the street in the line of horses, he saw the blanket butt of the Appaloosa horse. The Abbotts! They were still there.

A too-friendly arm slipped around his gun arm and her lavender perfume ran up his nose as he tried to think what he should do next. Then Thelma Van Doorne spoke in her deep, husky drawl.

"Slocum, you told me you were coming to play some games with me. What's taken you so long?"

He looked into her sky-blue eyes and then smiled. Hell with the Abbotts, hell with Jim Ed and the rest of the world.

"How far is your place?" he asked as he took her hand on his arm in his other hand and squeezed it. "I have been looking all over for you."

"That was the girl—"

"Yes, I just sent her home to her daddy."

"Tell me what you've been doing—"

He put a finger to her lips, glancing back down the street through the traffic to look for them. No sign of them, he hurried her on.

"Let's talk about you," he said, hurrying her along. "I've had a helluva rough time lately and I think anything you can tell me will be better."

She grinned at him and then she nodded with a wicked wink that she understood.

The following year, Slocum was in El Paso when the news broke that Broken Hand, as the Comanches called Mackenzie, captured the rest of the Kahwadie bands and Kiowas wintering in the secluded Palo Duro Canyon. He sat at a table in the Bloody Bucket Saloon and read the whole account by the reporter from Fort Worth who had accompanied Mackenzie.

Finished reading, he ordered another double whiskey and savored it. In the morning he was riding south. He had work guarding a gold mule train coming in from the

Sierra Madres. It beat swamping out bars and emptying spittoons. Someday he'd ride up there and examine this gorge that Barcelona Bill had spoken of. Must be some place. A cold shiver ran up his spine as he recalled how cold he had been the night Chief Green Horn died. Time to get moving. He set down the glass and left the barroom.

In the street he spotted the familiar horse. His white blanket dotted with black spots at the hitch rack in the yellow light spilled out of the bar down the street. Hell, they were there looking for him. He turned and went around the block for his horse at the livery. Mounted up, he crossed the shallow Rio Bravo a mile west of the bridge and rode south in the warm night.

There was a sweet gal in Tasco about twenty miles south. Juanita was her name. He looked back across the low greasewood bathed in moonlight. No one was coming. He rose in the stirrups and trotted the horse.

JAKE LOGAN
TODAY'S HOTTEST ACTION WESTERN!

__SLOCUM AT DOG LEG CREEK #199	0-515-11701-3/$3.99
__SLOCUM'S SILVER #200	0-515-11729-3/$3.99
__SLOCUM #201: RENEGADE TRAIL	0-515-11739-0/$4.50
__SLOCUM AND THE DIRTY GAME #202	0-515-11764-1/$4.50
__SLOCUM AND THE BEAR LAKE MONSTER #204	0-515-11806-0/$4.50
__SLOCUM AND THE APACHE RANSOM #209	0-515-11894-X/$4.99
__SLOCUM AT DEAD DOG #215	0-515-12015-4/$4.99
__SLOCUM AND THE TOWN BOSS #216	0-515-12030-8/$4.99
__SLOCUM AND THE LADY IN BLUE #217	0-515-12049-9/$4.99
__SLOCUM AND THE POWDER RIVER GAMBLE #218	0-515-12070-7/$4.99
__SLOCUM AND THE COLORADO RIVERBOAT #219	0-515-12081-2/$4.99
__SLOCUM #220: SLOCUM'S INHERITANCE	0-515-12103-7/$4.99
__SLOCUM AND DOC HOLLIDAY #221	0-515-12131-2/$4.99
__SLOCUM AND THE AZTEC PRIESTESS #222	0-515-12143-6/$4.99
__SLOCUM AND THE IRISH LASS (GIANT)	0-515-12155-X/$5.99
__SLOCUM AND THE COMANCHE RESCUE #223	0-515-12161-4/$4.99
__SLOCUM #224: LOUISIANA LOVELY (11/97)	0-515-12176-2/$4.99

Payable in U.S. funds. No cash accepted. Postage & handling: $1.75 for one book, 75¢ for each additional. Maximum postage $5.50. Prices, postage and handling charges may change without notice. Visa, Amex, MasterCard call 1-800-788-6262, ext. 1, or fax 1-201-933-2316; refer to ad #202d

Or, check above books   Bill my: ☐ Visa   ☐ MasterCard   ☐ Amex _____ (expires)
and send this order form to:
The Berkley Publishing Group   Card#_____

P.O. Box 12289, Dept. B   Daytime Phone #_____   ($10 minimum)
Newark, NJ 07101-5289   Signature_____

Please allow 4-6 weeks for delivery.   Or enclosed is my: ☐ check   ☐ money order
Foreign and Canadian delivery 8-12 weeks.

Ship to:

Name_____	Book Total	$_____
Address_____	Applicable Sales Tax (NY, NJ, PA, CA, GST Can.)	$_____
City_____	Postage & Handling	$_____
State/ZIP_____	Total Amount Due	$_____

Bill to: Name_____

Address_____ City_____
State/ZIP_____